HELL-O! I'M A LEMON-CELL-O!

Welcome, one and all, to the first of my Never-Bored Board Games, right here on Kidzapalooza—where kids rule! Today, these three intrepid teams will be writing their own stories inside my revolutionary new Fictionasium as they try to break out of my library!

Are you ready to go places you've never been before? Are you ready to become people you've never been before? Are you ready to break out of your comfort zones and break out of this library? Then on your mark! Get set! Lemon, cello, go!

PLAY ALL THE GAMES, SOLVE ALL THE PUZZLES— READ ALL THE LEMONCELLOS!

MR. LEMONCELLO'S

ALL-STAR
BREAKOUT
GAME

CHRIS
GRABENSTEIN

A Yearling Book

Text copyright © 2019 by Chris Grabenstein
Cover art copyright © 2020 by James Lancett

All rights reserved. Published in the United States by Yearling, an imprint of Random House Children's Books, a division of Penguin Random House LLC, New York. Originally published in hardcover in the United States by Random House Children's Books, a division of Penguin Random House LLC, New York, in 2019.

Yearling and the jumping horse design are registered trademarks of Penguin Random House LLC.

Visit us on the Web! rhcbooks.com

Educators and librarians, for a variety of teaching tools, visit us at RHTeachersLibrarians.com

The Library of Congress has cataloged the hardcover edition of this work as follows:
Name: Grabenstein, Chris, author.
Title: Mr. Lemoncello's all-star breakout game / Chris Grabenstein.
Description: First edition. | New York: Random House, [2019] | Sequel to: Mr. Lemoncello's great library race. | Summary: "To win Mr. Lemoncello's new television game show, Kyle and his team have to break out of their comfort zone and walk a mile in other characters' shoes and figure out how to unlock a series of locks and break out of the game before their competition!"
—Provided by publisher.
Identifiers: LCCN 2018007935 | ISBN 978-0-525-64644-0 (hardcover) | ISBN 978-0-525-64645-7 (library binding) | ISBN 978-0-525-64646-4 (ebook)
Subjects: | CYAC: Game shows—Fiction. | Contests—Fiction. | Libraries—Fiction. | Books and reading—Fiction. | Eccentrics and eccentricities—Fiction. | Friendship—Fiction.
Classification: LCC PZ7.G7487 Mh 2019 | DDC [Fic]—dc23

ISBN 978-0-525-64647-1 (pbk.)

Printed in the United States of America
10 9 8 7 6 5 4 3 2 1
First Yearling Edition 2020

*For my seventh-grade English teacher,
Mrs. June P. Garret, who wrote in the margins of one of
my homework assignments these words of encouragement:
"You will make your living as a writer someday."*

"I love this wacky game!" shouted Kyle Keeley.

He probably shouldn't've been shouting, because he was in the middle school library playing video games with his friends Akimi Hughes, Sierra Russell, and Miguel Fernandez.

Actually, he probably shouldn't've been playing games on a library computer, either. This was supposed to be his "independent reading" time.

But just the night before, while watching his former classmate Haley Daley's new TV show, *Hey, Hey, Haley,* on the Kidzapalooza Network, Kyle had seen a commercial for Mr. Lemoncello's new What Else Do You See? It was an online puzzle game filled with fast-flipping, high-flying animated optical illusions.

Was it fun? "Fun?" Haley chirped at the end of the commercial. "Hell-o? It's a Lemon-cell-o!"

Kyle just had to try it. As soon as possible! (Which turned out to be "independent reading" time.)

"This is level one," he said as a puzzler popped onto the screen with a ticking ten-second countdown clock.

"Easy," said Akimi, typing as fast as she could on the keyboard. "A vase and two faces. Or a candlestick. That vase could be a candlestick."

"It's a classic," said Sierra, who was something of a bookworm and brainiac. "Optical illusions are an excellent tool for studying visual perception."

"Or, you know, having fun," said Kyle.

Akimi hit return. The screen exploded into pixelated confetti, which settled to spell out "Congratulicitations!"

"Let's move up to level two!" said Akimi, eager for more.

"You guys?" said Miguel, glancing toward the librarian. (He was president of the school's Library Aide Society.) "We should probably go back to reading our books. . . ."

"In a minute," said Kyle, clacking the keyboard. A fresh optical illusion appeared: a road sign. The timer started counting down from ten again.

"That's just Idaho," said Miguel. He couldn't resist the lure of a Lemoncello game, even though he knew he should. "See? 'I-D-A-H-O'!"

"What about an old guy?" asked Kyle.

"Nope," said Akimi. "It's just Idaho."

She hit enter.

A buzzer *SCRONK*ed.

"Okay. My bad."

"Do the next one!" urged Sierra.

Sierra Russell never used to get all that excited playing games. But then she met Kyle Keeley and the legendary game maker Luigi L. Lemoncello.

Kyle clicked the mouse. Up came a new image and a new ten-second timer.

"A woman's face!" said Sierra.

"Nope," said Akimi. "A saxophone player with a ginormous nose. No, wait. You're right. It's a woman's face. Nope. Saxophone player with a big nose . . ."

"It all depends on how you look at it," said Miguel.

"Type in 'woman'!" said Sierra.

"Nope," said Kyle. " 'Saxophone dude.' "

" 'Woman'!" shouted Miguel. "No. Wait. Both!"

One more thing Kyle and his friends probably shouldn't've been doing? Talking so loudly.

Because Mrs. Yunghans, the middle school librarian, strolled over to see what all the noise was about.

And Charles Chiltington was right behind her.

"I thought you four were back here reading books," said Mrs. Yunghans, sounding disappointed in the students who had made her a school-librarian legend by winning so many games inside Mr. Lemoncello's library.

"I know that's precisely what I was doing, Mrs. Yunghans," said Charles. He was always super polite in front of adults. "And, if I may, I now understand why *The Red Badge of Courage* by Stephen Crane is considered to be such an abiding, archetypical, and ageless classic."

Charles also liked to use big words. The more the merrier.

"You know you just said the same thing three times, right?" said Akimi.

"Well, at least I wasn't playing mindless video games, as you miscreants and ne'er-do-wells indubitably were."

Charles Chiltington (and his family) had been out to

get Kyle and his friends ever since Kyle's idol, the genius game maker Luigi Lemoncello, had returned to his hometown of Alexandriaville, Ohio, to build the most spectacular, technologically advanced, and awesometastic library ever built anywhere. So far, Charles had been embarrassed every time he tried to beat them at the library, so now he was trying to defeat them at school.

Mrs. Yunghans shook her head. "It is so sad to see you, my four library superstars, playing video games instead of reading books. *Et tu,* Sierra?"

"That's from Shakespeare, isn't it, Mrs. Yunghans?" said Charles.

"Yes. *Julius Caesar.*"

"My, you certainly are extremely well read. That must be why you're such an excellent librarian."

"Thank you, Charles."

"But, Mrs. Yunghans," said Kyle, "this isn't any ordinary video game. Hell-o? It's a Lemon-cell-o!" He tried to trill it like Haley did in the commercials.

It wasn't working.

"Mr. Keeley?" The librarian gave Kyle a look that made his dimples wither.

"Yes, ma'am?"

"There's a time and a place for everything."

"So true," said Charles. "And might I just add, this is definitely the time and place for me to admire your sweater-vest! It's so incredibly well crafted. Did you knit it yourself, Mrs. Yunghans?"

"Why, yes, I did. Now, where was I?"

"I believe you were just about to issue Kyle, Akimi, Miguel, and, sadly, even Sierra three detentions each," said Charles.

"Wha-hut?" gasped Akimi. "Three?"

"I've never had even one detention before," said Sierra.

"And why was I about to do that?" said Mrs. Yunghans.

"Because," said Charles, "these students were disobeying your direct orders to read a book, while using library computers to play"—he put his fist to his lips like he might be ill—"a video game!"

Mrs. Yunghans sighed. "I'm sorry, guys. I expect more from you as role models." She picked up a pen and a pink pad.

A detention meant they'd have to stay an hour after school.

"Mrs. Yunghans?" said Kyle.

"Yes, Kyle?"

"This was my fault. I'm the one who downloaded the game. I'm the one who convinced everybody else to quit reading and start playing. Akimi, Miguel, and Sierra were only breaking the rules because of me. Give me the three detentions. I earned them. But these guys are innocent."

"I admire your honesty, Kyle," said the librarian.

"Kyle should get five detentions instead of three!" blurted Charles.

"Explain your math," demanded Akimi.

7

"Easy. He admits he was the agitator. The rabble-rousing ringleader. The chief mischief-maker."

Akimi rolled her eyes. "You do know you're saying the same thing over and over, right?"

"Because it needs to be said! Let the punishment fit the crime, Mrs. Yunghans. If you don't, you're paving the path to anarchy!"

Mrs. Yunghans considered what Charles had said. "Charles is correct, Kyle. Playing video games on library computers during reading time?"

She shook her head and turned the "3" on the pad into a "5" with a sideways flick of her pen.

Kyle would be staying after school for five days—a whole school week.

Charles smirked. In their never-ending competition, he had just pulled ahead of Kyle by slamming him with a dreaded "Go to Detention" card.

And there was nothing Kyle could do about it.

At least not on this turn!

3

Five seconds later, the bell rang.

Kyle and his friends gathered up their stuff. Charles stayed back with the librarian.

"If you have a free moment, Mrs. Yunghans, I'd love to discuss making a few changes to the Library Aide Society. Miguel has been president for so long. He's done an acceptable job, I suppose, but you and I both know we could do better. . . ."

"Um, I'm right here, Chiltington," said Miguel. "I can hear you."

Charles ignored him. "Let me help you reshelve those books. . . ."

Pushing a library cart loaded down with book returns, Charles disappeared into the stacks with Mrs. Yunghans.

"Dudes?" said Miguel, shaking his head. "I officially hate that guy."

* * *

"I don't know what I'm going to tell my parents," said Kyle when he and his friends regrouped in the cafeteria for lunch. Andrew Peckleman joined them.

"I wouldn't tell them if I were you," suggested Andrew, talking through his nose and adjusting his goggle-sized glasses. "Telling them would just be stupid."

"Can you believe the way Chiltington was trash-talking me?" said Miguel.

"He's such a suck-up," said Akimi.

"You guys," said Sierra, chewing her lip. "Maybe there's something about Charles that we're missing. Some reason he acts the way he does."

"You mean like a jerk?" said Kyle.

"Easy," said Akimi. "His jerkiness combined with his jerkitude and jerkosity."

"Have any of you read *To Kill a Mockingbird*?" Sierra asked.

"It's in my TBR pile," said Kyle, who had the tallest stack of books to be read of any of his friends.

"Well, it's like Atticus says to Scout: 'You never really understand a person until you consider things from his point of view . . . until you climb into his skin and walk around in it.'"

"Walk around in Charles Chiltington's skin?" said Miguel. "Gross."

"The guy's such a slimy snake," said Kyle, "he probably sheds his skin on a regular basis."

Everybody at the table cracked up.

But Kyle knew Charles would have the last laugh. When school was over, Kyle would have to report to room 101.

Detention. The time-out box on the board game called middle school.

Fortunately, detention only lasted an hour. He'd still be home in plenty of time to catch *The Buzz Show* on Kidzapalooza. It was only a five-minute program. Mostly gossip and news about movies, music, fads, and celebrities. Haley Daley, who grew up in Alexandriaville and had competed in the very first escape game at Mr. Lemoncello's library, was on it all the time. So were other Kidzapalooza stars, like Kai Kumar, Gabrielle Grande, Peyton McCallister, and everybody's favorite cooltastic dude, Jaylen Swell.

But today, there'd be an extra-special guest on *Buzz:* Mr. Luigi L. Lemoncello.

Rumor had it, Mr. L was all set to make some sort of major announcement.

Probably about a new game.

And Kyle was going to be home in time to watch it—no matter what!

4

"Nerd!" jeered Charles.

He'd positioned himself outside room 101 after the final bell rang. "Enjoy detention. Have fun with all the other losers, Keeley."

"We're not losers," said a tough-looking girl. She was about six feet tall and appeared to be a detention regular.

"I didn't mean you," Charles replied meekly. "I was referring to *that* loser. Kyle Keeley."

Keeley didn't respond. He simply shook his head and headed into the room to do his time.

Charles giggled.

He was having such a delightful day. That night at dinner, he'd be sure to tell his father how he had crushed the competition at school. If his father came home from the office in time. Charles's father was a very busy man. His time wasn't his own.

Many nights, Charles and his mother dined alone. Of course, the servants were there. But they didn't really count. They weren't Chiltingtons.

While they dined, Charles and his mother often commiserated about the Lemoncello library.

They both hated the place.

"It's dangerous, demented, and disgusting," his mother would always say. "They lend out too many of the wrong sorts of books. Someone needs to stand up to that lunatic Luigi and shut him down once and for all."

Charles agreed. In fact, he and his mother had been trying to run Mr. Lemoncello out of town ever since he hosted his ridiculous Library Olympics.

"How was your day, Charles?" his mother asked when he arrived home. The cook was with her, holding a glass of chilled milk and a china plate bearing two freshly baked chocolate chip cookies.

Charles glared at the cookies. "Chocolate chip? *Again?* I told you, Mother, I wanted peanut butter cookies today!"

"I'm so sorry, Charles. Isabella is sorry, too. Aren't you, Isabella?"

The cook nodded. Her hands were trembling so much, jiggling cookie crumbs danced around the dainty plate.

"And, Isabella," said Charles, "I want chunks of peanut butter cups baked into my peanut butter cookies! Is that clear?"

"Oh, what a marvelous idea, Charles!" said his mother. "Peanut butter cookies with chunks of peanut butter cups!

You certainly are creative. An inspiration to pastry chefs everywhere!"

Charles grinned. Score another victory. A small one, perhaps, but every victory counted.

"I'll be in my room watching TV," he told his mother.

"Don't you have homework, dear?"

"Nothing that one of my tutors can't email me later this evening. I am not to be disturbed for any reason except cookie delivery."

"Of course, dear."

Charles marched up the curving staircase to the second floor, entered his thickly carpeted bedroom, and flicked on the giant-screen TV. It was tuned to the Kidzapalooza Network, Charles's favorite. He especially liked Kai Kumar's acrobatic antics on an obstacle-course game show called *Sludge Dodgers*. Kai was always tripping, toppling, slipping, and being slimed.

The gangly guy knew how to play a loser. And any loser, even a funny one on TV, always made Charles feel more like a winner.

"Hey, hey, hello!" chirped a perky voice the instant the set powered up.

It was Haley Daley, the middle school cheerleader from Alexandriaville who had somehow double-crossed (some would say outsmarted) Charles in the original escape game at the Lemoncello library.

The girl his father admired so, so much. "Haley Daley is a real winner," he said all the time. "She knew how to pull herself up by her bootstraps. You could learn from her, Charles."

Charles always promised he'd try.

Haley's on-screen smile was dazzling. "I hope you'll be watching *Hey, Hey, Haley* tonight at eight, only on Kidzapalooza—where kids rule!"

An arm reached in from off camera and thumped a pie in her face. Haley comically cleaned the whipped cream away from her eyes and mouth until it looked like she was wearing a marshmallow mask. "Hey, hey!" she said in mock shock. "Who threw this banana cream pie at me? I ordered chocolate!"

The screen cut to spinning, bouncing graphics promoting her new show's airtime.

Of all the so-called winners of the rigged games at Mr. Lemoncello's library, Haley had come out on top. After appearing in Mr. Lemoncello's holiday commercials (the prize for winning the escape game), she'd moved out to Hollywood with her family and started doing guest appearances in sitcoms on the Disney Channel.

She'd also landed a singing contract and recorded an album, *Gummi Worms 'n' Bubble Gum,* which went double platinum.

Now she was starring in her own TV show on Kidzapalooza.

Haley Daley was bigger than Kyle Keeley could ever hope to be.

Charles only wished he could, somehow, become a TV

star. It would be the ultimate victory. It would prove to his father that *he* was a winner, too!

Another promo splashed across the screen: "Hey, gang, be sure to check out *The Buzz Show* tonight at seven, when Mr. Luigi L. Lemoncello, the genius game maker behind all things Lemoncello, will tell us about something big coming from his Imagination Factory *and* Kidzapalooza. You won't want to miss it."

"Speak for yourself!" shouted Charles, hurling the remote across the room.

How he despised Mr. Lemoncello, his library, and his games! The old fool had conspired to cheat Charles out of what was rightfully his.

"Mr. Lemoncello made you look like a loser, Charles, in front of the whole town" was how his father put it. "And Chiltingtons never lose! Especially not in front of our neighbors!"

Charles, of course, would tune in at seven to see what loony Mr. Lemoncello had to say.

"You need to size up your competition, find their weaknesses," his father always told him. Then his dad would quote from the famous Chinese general Sun Tzu's *Art of War:* "To know your enemy, you must become your enemy."

5

"You will soon become the star of this video game, Dr. Z,"
said Mr. Lemoncello as he typed a series of commands on
a keyboard.

He was behind the fiction wall at his library with his
head librarian, Dr. Yanina Zinchenko, and head imagineer, Chester Raymo. They were working around the
clock, test-driving his most exciting invention ever—one
that had to be "ready for prime time" in two weeks.

"Slay that dragon, Dr. Z!" shouted Mr. Lemoncello,
bopping the return button.

"I can't, sir. There's a troll blocking me."

"Why not ask if it's friendly?"

"Doubtful, sir. Trolls seldom are. However, this one *is*
riding a unicorn."

"Yes, I can see that on my monitor. Allow me, your

masterful story master, to add one more character! A narwhal!"

Mr. Lemoncello clicked another series of keys on the Narrative Drive—a mainframe computer linked to multiple holographic projectors and remote controllers for audio-animatronic dummies, all set up inside a maze of darkened rooms. Mr. Lemoncello called the newest addition to his high-tech library the Fictionasium because the rooms allowed visitors to become characters inside fictional stories. Just like in Dungeons and Dragons, a story master set the scene. The players created the plot.

"Fiction is amazible!" Mr. Lemoncello cried out. "There are no limits. It's where the mountain meets the moon! This will be our most incredible game ever. Perfect for TV!"

Dr. Zinchenko, the world-famous librarian, was testing one of the Fictionasium rooms. She wore a black motion capture suit—what people in Hollywood called a MoCap suit. It was like a leotard with white Ping-Pong balls Velcroed to pivot points on the arms, legs, and torso. Her head was covered with a snug black hood that exposed only her facial features. The MoCap suit allowed cameras to track her movements and, through the marvels of computer-generated imagery, or CGI, costume her appropriately for any interactive story.

Scenery projected on the walls made the experience inside the story seem hyperrealistic for the players. So did the floating holograms.

The players could see the full effect of all the technological wizardry—the computer-generated special effects mixed with the live action, the holograms, and the robotic mannequins—on ninety-five-inch video monitors mounted on all four walls of each Fictionasium room.

They could watch themselves inside the story they were helping to create.

"The narwhal is flapping its flippers at me, sir," Dr. Zinchenko reported in her thick Russian accent. "What shall I do next?"

"Ah, that is up to you, Dr. Z! Inside the Fictionasium, you must write your own stories."

"Doing my best in here, sir." She glanced up at her image on the nearest video screen. "However, I have never actually been a fairy-tale princess before."

"Simply put yourself in her twinkly shoes, Yanina!"

"Very well," said Dr. Zinchenko, pausing for a moment to ponder her next move. "Greetings, narwhal friend," she called out.

"Welcome to the North Pole!" said the narwhal. "How may I help you?"

"That troll riding the unicorn is blocking my shot at the dragon."

"How may I help you?" said the narwhal. Again.

"You must give it a command!" coached Mr. Lemoncello.

"Narwhal!" cried Dr. Zinchenko as regally as she

could. "Kindly attack yon unicorn with your glimmering horn!"

"As you wish!" replied the narwhal. It charged across the room and head-butted the unicorn's rear end. The unicorn popped, yelped, and shrank like a punctured balloon spewing sparkle powder.

"Arrgggh!" grumbled the hairy troll, sliding off the unicorn's saddle. "The unicorn is deflated and I am defeated."

The troll trundled away.

"Take out the dragon!" coached the narwhal. "Only you can slay it, DR. ZINCHENKO."

The narwhal vanished, leaving Dr. Z face to face with an angry dragon. The holographic creature reared up on its haunches and took in a deep, fire-stoking breath.

Dr. Zinchenko grabbed a pair of long-handled dust mops conveniently lying on the floor and tickled the beast's belly.

The dragon began to giggle and jiggle.

"Well done, Dr. Z!" shouted Mr. Lemoncello. "You *will* be advancing to the next level. You made the dragon laugh."

"I believe I also made it fart uncontrollably, sir. I smell rotten eggs. Several dozen."

"Smell-a-vision! Isn't it fantabulous?"

Dr. Zinchenko fanned the foul air under her nose. "Sometimes, sir. Sometimes."

Chester Raymo, Mr. Lemoncello's head imagineer,

emerged from the shadows. His eyes were watering from the stench.

"Suggest we override this scenario, sir. Immediately."

"Right you are, Chet," said Mr. Lemoncello. "I'm expecting a very important call from my friends at Kidzapalooza! I can't be distracted by dragon farts!"

6

"Goodness gracious gollywhoppers," huffed Mr. Lemoncello, "this room smells worse than the Stinky Cheese Man's birthday party with the week-old Gorgonzola cake. Mr. Raymo, let's write a quick 'The End' to this story before it ends all of us!"

"Good idea, sir. There are bugs in the system. It is not ready for TV—"

"Nonsense!" said Mr. Lemoncello. With a swirling flourish, he pulled a key that looked like a scrolled letter "L" out of his waistcoat. Mr. Raymo yanked a similar key out of his white lab coat. Both keys had glistening microchips embedded in their teeth.

"Simultaneously insert two keys into the room's control box," said Mr. Raymo. "Twist right to alter scenario."

They turned their keys—hard to the right. Mr. Raymo tapped a series of commands onto the tablet computer attached to the top of the box. With a loud electronic thump, the magical world vanished. The air in the room instantly deodorized itself. The fantasy room was just a black box with a grid of pipes and lights and projectors suspended overhead.

"Well, Dr. Zinchenko," boomed Mr. Lemoncello, "was it fun?"

"Fun?" she said. "Hello? It's a Lemoncello!"

"I know," said Mr. Lemoncello. "So am I. But I'd still love to have one of the kids give the Fictionasium a trial run."

"It's not ready!" insisted Mr. Raymo.

Mr. Lemoncello brushed off the warning. "Tut-tut. Have we heard from Kyle Keeley today?"

"Yes, sir," reported Dr. Zinchenko. "Unfortunately, he won't be able to join us this evening. He was detained in detention."

"Oh, dear," said Mr. Lemoncello. "What happened?"

"According to his text, and I quote, 'It was all that creep Charles Chiltington's fault.' "

"Hmm. We must, someday, find a happier ending to their sad saga—"

Suddenly, Mr. Lemoncello's top hat started to *DING-DONG-DING-DONG!* like a pealing church bell.

"Excuse me," he said, his teeth chattering. "I'd better answer that. It's my head phone."

He reached up and tapped the flat top of his hat. It popped open. Reaching inside, he extracted an old-fashioned telephone receiver connected to a coiled yellow cord.

He put the phone to his ear.

"Yello? This is Luigi L. Lemoncello. To whom do I have the pleasure of speaking?"

He listened for a moment, then placed his hand over the mouthpiece.

"It's Buzz from the Kidzapalooza Network!" he whispered to Dr. Zinchenko and Mr. Raymo. "He wants me to say a few exciting words about our upcoming game for this evening's episode of his show. Huzzah!"

He put the phone back to his ear.

"Very well, Buzz. Here come a few exciting words. 'Thrilling,' 'exhilarating,' and 'electrifying,' all of which can be used to describe the greatest event in the history of television game shows: *Mr. Lemoncello's All-Star Breakout Game*!"

He covered the phone with his hand again.

"Mr. Raymo? Fire up the nearest video camera and start recording my every word. I'm going to be on TV! Tonight!"

"Oh, man!" said Kyle. "This is so huge!"

He and his brothers, Mike and Curtis, were in the family room, watching TV. It was seven o'clock. Mr. Lemoncello's prerecorded announcement was playing on Kidzapalooza's *Buzz Show*.

"Why's he talking into that yellow telephone?" wondered Mike.

"Maybe he couldn't find a microphone," said Curtis.

"That's his head phone," said Kyle. "Now be quiet, you guys. I need to hear this!"

"It will be the greatest event in the history of television game shows!" said Mr. Lemoncello. "My first-ever *All-Star Breakout Game*."

"Guess that means you won't get to play," said Mike, who was on the county's football *and* baseball all-star teams. "You're not an all-star, Kyle."

"Technically," said Curtis, "he is. He starred in all those TV commercials."

"And all the other games at the library!" added Kyle.

"It's not the same thing as playing football!" said Mike. "Or baseball."

"I know," said Kyle with a grin. "It's better."

"Tell us about this new game, Mr. L," said Buzz Binkley, the host of *The Buzz Show* on Kidzapalooza.

"With pleasure, Buzz," said Mr. Lemoncello, his smiling face filling the TV screen.

Kyle felt as if Mr. L were talking directly to him and nobody else!

"It will be broadcast live from my library's brand-new Fictionasium. And I can guaran-double-tee you and your viewers that the game will be filled with action, adventure, and surprises, or my name isn't Luigi Lemoncello, which, I assure you, it is, because years ago, before I went to summer camp, my mother sewed name tags into my underpants. Stay tuned to Kidzapalooza for more details! About the game show. Not my underpants."

Mr. Lemoncello didn't mention who the contestants might be.

But Kyle would do whatever it took to make sure he was one of them!

* * *

Meanwhile, on the other side of town, Charles Chiltington was watching *The Buzz Show* announcement on the sixty-five-inch screen of his bedroom TV.

"No one wants to hear about your droopy underpants, you doddering old fool!" Charles hissed at the television.

"This is going to be a super, major, enormopendous event," Mr. Lemoncello told his Kidzapalooza host. "Why, it'll be bigger than the day the crayons quit because we'll be live, in millions of homes, in America and all around the globe."

"Where will you find your contestants?" asked Buzz.

"Well, to be honest, we're under a bit of a time crunch, which, by the way, would be an excellent name for a sugary cereal shaped like tiny pocket watches. We won't be able to do a nationwide talent search—not for this first game, anyway. I'm going to be looking for ten contestants right here in my hometown, at the middle school in Alexandriaville, Ohio!"

Interesting, thought Charles. *Another game limited to students attending Alexandriaville Middle School, just like Mr. Lemoncello's original escape game.*

That meant Charles was, once again, eligible to play.

He could become the next big TV star.

This might be exactly what Charles needed to prove to his father once and for all that he was a true Chiltington. That he was a winner.

"Thank you for taking the time to be with us today," said Buzz.

"My pleasure!" said Mr. Lemoncello, turning to face the camera. "And to the kids back home in Alexandriaville? I hope you're ready to play!"

He tossed the phone he'd been speaking into up in the air. The cord stretched itself into a taut line and then, coils reasserting themselves, snapped back into the top hat. The lid flapped shut like a reverse jack-in-the-box.

"Awesome!" said Kyle.

"Ridiculous!" said Charles.

But both of them were thinking the same thing: They really, really, *really* wanted to play (and win) *Mr. Lemoncello's All-Star Breakout Game*!

8

"So, did you catch Mr. Lemoncello on *The Buzz Show* last night?" Kyle asked Akimi the next morning.

They were heading up the hall to homeroom.

"Of course," said Akimi. "And did you tell your parents about your detentions?"

"Not really."

"What does that mean?"

"I'm waiting for the right moment."

"And when will that be?"

"Sometime after we play this new All-Star Breakout Game! It's going to be on TV, Akimi. Live! That means it'll be bigger than the escape, Olympics, and race games combined."

"You really should tell them," said Akimi.

"I will. Someday."

Kyle and Akimi walked into Mrs. Cameron's room.

They saw Charles Chiltington dressed in his khaki pants, blue blazer, white shirt, and striped tie. He was the only kid at Alexandriaville Middle School who dressed as if the place were an Ivy League prep school.

Charles was buttering up Mrs. Cameron. Again.

"Did you know, Mrs. Cameron, that your first name, Dana, means 'knowledgeable' in Persian? It's no wonder you're such an excellent teacher."

"Why, thank you, Charles."

Akimi turned to Kyle and did one of her famous "gag me now" gestures.

"Speaking of knowledge," Charles continued, "do you know anything more about this new Lemoncello TV game show? The one he announced on Kidzapalooza last night?"

"I'm afraid not, Charles," replied Mrs. Cameron.

The second bell rang and everybody took their seats.

"All right, class," said Mrs. Cameron. "It's time for the morning announcements."

Alexandriaville Middle School did announcements like a morning news show, broadcasting from a studio set up inside the library.

Alexandra Paisley and Joshua Bernheisel, two eighth graders, were the co-anchors of WAMS.

Mrs. Cameron aimed her remote at the video monitor mounted on the wall. Familiar news music came pounding out of the speakers. A spinning graphic that read "Breaking News" swirled onto the screen. It faded away. Alexandra and Joshua appeared.

30

"Breaking news!" said Joshua. "We have a special guest in the studio this morning."

"That's right," said Alexandra. "He parked his boot-mobile in the parking lot. He burp-squeaked his banana shoes up the hallways and into our studio. His favorite chicken dish is Artemis Fowl."

"Yep," said Joshua. "You guessed it. It's the one, the only . . ."

The two anchors said the next line together: "Luigi L. Lemoncello!"

"Woo-hoo!" shouted Kyle, Akimi, and every other kid in the room (except Charles).

The camera widened out. Mr. Lemoncello, wearing his top hat, checkerboard vest, and bright yellow tailcoat, rolled across the frame in an office chair.

Judging by the crash and clatter of metal on metal, he hit something two seconds after he glided out of the frame on the other side.

"Oopsy," he said offscreen. "My bad."

Mr. Lemoncello's shoes burp-squeaked as he gave himself a quick shove and rolled back into the frame. This time, he slammed on the burp-squeak brakes and parked beside the two eighth graders.

"Guess I'll never be a roller girl," he said with a wink. He curled the ends of his white mustache to tidy them up. Then he tipped his hat at Joshua and Alexandra.

"Hearty and splendiferous greetings to you both."

"Great to have you here, Mr. L," said Alexandra. "Can

you tell us about this exciting new game show on Kidzapalooza?"

"Maybe."

"Huh?"

"Well, not to be mysterious like the Benedict Society, but to play my new game, you'll have to be able to solve puzzles like . . . this!"

Mr. Lemoncello reached into his coat and whipped out a rebus mounted on a poster board.

The camera pushed in. A string of graphics filled the frame.

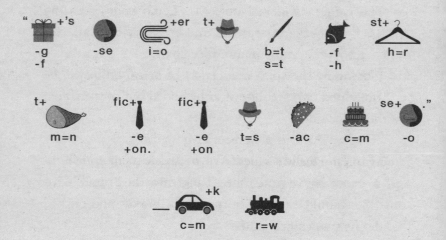

"Boys and girls," said Mr. Lemoncello, "if you can solve this perplexing and befuddling brainteaser, you might be exactly the middle school students I'm looking for to star in my brand-new TV game show on Kidzapalooza!"

9

Unbelievable! thought Kyle.

It was really happening. A whole new game. The chance to win again—at the library *and* on TV in front of millions. Kyle had to, had to, *had to* be on the show.

He was scribbling furiously, decoding the rebus puzzle as rapidly as he could. His big brother Mike was an all-star jock. His brother Curtis was an all-star brainiac. Puzzles, riddles, and games? *This* was where Kyle outshone them both.

He looked over at Charles, who was also working as fast as he could to decode the rebus.

So Kyle scribbled faster.

On the TV screen, Joshua Bernheisel and Alexandra Paisley were working the puzzle together on a yellow legal pad. Mr. Lemoncello held a pocket watch the size of an alarm clock in his hand. Its ticktocking second hand was extremely noisy.

Kyle finished the puzzle and slammed down his pen—just half a second before Charles slammed down his. Everybody else in the classroom was still scratching their heads or scratching out an answer.

"*ZONK!*" said Mr. Lemoncello, becoming a human buzzer. "Time's up!" He flipped his clue card over to reveal the answer.

"It's no wonder that truth is stranger than fiction.

Fiction has to make sense."

—Mark Twain

"Yes!" Kyle arm-pumped. "Nailed it."

He fist-bumped Akimi.

"I suspect you made a lucky guess," scoffed Charles.

"What'd you write down?"

"Nothing," said Charles, turning over his worksheet so no one could see his answer. "I find Mr. Lemoncello's games to be an immature and foolish waste of time."

"Now, for those of you who don't find my games to be an immature and foolish waste of time," said Mr. Lemoncello on the TV, "I invite you to become players in my All-Star Breakout Game. My library will be the playing board. Ten of you will become playing pieces. That's right. I'm looking for two teams of five players each. We will be recruiting those teams right here, immediately after school!"

"Woo-hoo!" shouted Kyle.

He and Akimi knocked knuckles again.

"Teammates?" said Akimi.

"Definitely," said Kyle. He looked over at Charles, who was suddenly laser-focused on everything Mr. Lemoncello said.

"Confer with your friends, create your teams, and then come to the game show auditions this afternoon in the auditorium."

"What's the game about?" asked Joshua.

"Oh, about two hours," said Mr. Lemoncello. "That includes commercials, of course."

"But what's the point of the game?" asked Alexandra.

"Ah! Good point. I forgot to point out the point. This game will be played inside the Lemoncello library's brand-new Fictionasium. You, the players, will go on interactive adventures to rival those of Greg Heffley, Captain Underpants, and Auggie Pullman. For this game, you will need more than puzzle-solving or research-digging skills as you work your way through a maze of literary genres. In every room you enter, stories will spring to life, and you will become the main characters! Solve the riddles, find the clues, overcome the obstacles, and you might be the first to break out of the library and emerge victorious!"

"What's the prize?" asked Joshua.

"The best ever, and I'm not joshing, Joshua. One member of the winning team will be selected to host their own Lemoncello game show on Kidzapalooza!"

"*YES!*" said Kyle. And Charles. At the exact same time.

"Their teammates will be the first contestants!"

"TV!" said Charles, halfway under his breath.

That caught Kyle's attention. Charles pointed two fingers at his eyeballs and then at Kyle and then back at his eyes.

"Thanks for dropping by, Mr. Lemoncello," said Alexandra.

"My pleasure!" Mr. Lemoncello turned to the camera. "And I hope to see all of you after school today at the auditions!"

Mr. Lemoncello waved goodbye and rolled off camera.

He also, apparently, crashed into some more lights and video equipment.

Kyle felt like crashing into something, too. He was that excited!

The WAMS morning news show wrapped up with the Pledge of Allegiance. Mrs. Cameron said some homeroomy stuff that Kyle barely heard, the bell rang, and Kyle met up in the halls with his Lemoncello library pals: Akimi, Miguel, Sierra, and Andrew.

"So, do you guys think this new game will be about books?" asked Kyle.

"Uh, yeah," said Akimi. "Duh."

"But what kind?"

"Judging by the characters Mr. Lemoncello listed," said Sierra, "this new game will most likely be dealing with fiction."

"Makes sense," said Miguel. "Because the Fabulous

Fact-Finding Frenzy was all about nonfiction. This new breakout game will be about fiction."

"And we get to play the characters," said Akimi. "It'll be like those Choose Your Own Adventure books."

"I love those," said Miguel.

"I usually end up dying," sighed Andrew.

"Not this time, Andrew," Kyle promised. "This time you're on our team!"

They all slapped a noisy high five.

"Booyah!"

10

That morning, right after homeroom, Charles's phone buzzed.

It was a text from his father with the Lemoncello All-Star Breakout Game news alert attached.

> Here's another chance to redeem yourself, son. If you win this game on TV, in front of millions, it will erase all your previous defeats.

His father was, of course, correct. If Charles could defeat Keeley on national TV, it would wipe away all of Charles's past losses. A few thousand people knew about those. *Millions* would learn of his victory if it was broadcast on TV.

It was like Dr. Seuss wrote in that book one of Charles's nannies used to read to him: "*Fame!* You'll be famous as famous can be, with the whole wide world watching you win on TV!"

"This time, I won't let you down, Father," Charles vowed. "I will emerge victorious!"

There was only one problem. Mr. Lemoncello had just declared that this was to be a team sport. Charles preferred to fly solo. Plus, unlike his archrival, Kyle Keeley, he did not have a ready-made circle of friends to turn into an instant team for the new game.

So, before he could become famous, Charles needed to cobble together a team of all-stars. And he needed to do it fast. As one of his father's favorite Sun Tzu *Art of War* quotes put it, "Quickness is the essence of war!"

Charles decided to consult Mrs. Yunghans. Surely the librarian could help him select the fiercest fiction readers in the school.

During his free period, he took her a cinnamon dolce latte he'd had delivered from a nearby coffee shop.

"Well, aren't you sweet, Charles!" she gushed when he brought her the drink, topped with whipped cream and chocolate sprinkles.

"Mrs. Yunghans? Might I ask you a hypothetical question?"

"Certainly."

"If I were to put together a team to compete in this new Lemoncello breakout game, whom would you suggest I invite to play with me?"

"Well," she said, "you definitely want Sierra Russell on your team."

"She's not available."

"Then I'd ask Miguel Fernandez."

"Unavailable."

"Andrew Peckleman?"

"Unavailable."

"Oh, right. Of course. They'll all be on Kyle's team. Well, I think I'd ask some of the eighth graders."

Oh, thought Charles. *Smart.* Keeley and his companions were seventh graders. So was Charles. But Mr. Lemoncello had opened up this new competition to the entire middle school. Fielding a team of eighth graders would be a brilliant strategy. They'd all be one year smarter than Keeley's players.

"Which eighth graders should I pursue most aggressively?" he asked.

Mrs. Yunghans sipped her latte. "Mmm. Delish."

Charles smiled. And blinked. And waited.

"Okay," said Mrs. Yunghans, wiping whipped cream off her lip. "Eighth graders. You definitely want Morgan Peden. She's an even bigger bookworm than Sierra Russell."

Charles scribbled the name in his notebook. "Perfect. Who else?"

"Ryan Capruso," said Mrs. Yunghans. "He's read everything J. R. R. Tolkien ever wrote. And those books are thick."

"Excellent. Two more?"

"Mirabai Keshap and Hannah Chung. They're co-captains of this year's eighth-grade Battle of the Books team."

"Thank you, Mrs. Yunghans. If you see Morgan, Ryan, Mirabai, or Hannah before I do, please let them know of my interest in recruiting them."

"Of course. But, if I may, why would eighth graders elect to be on a team captained by a seventh grader?"

"Because, Mrs. Yunghans, I am a Chiltington. And Chiltingtons never lose."

"Really? Because in the escape game—"

"I will also provide gift cards and an introduction to my father, who is someone who can make big things happen for them! After all, he is the wealthiest man in town."

"Except for Mr. Lemoncello."

"Right," said Charles, forcing the smile to stay stretched across his face. "Except for him."

By lunchtime, after some serious negotiating and the promise of summer jobs, the four eighth graders had all said yes.

Charles marched into the cafeteria with his newly recruited teammates, feeling giddy.

Hannah Chung had a board game box tucked under her arm.

"We can get into a proper Lemoncello mind-set by playing his Fantabulous Floating Emoji game during lunch," she suggested.

"An excellent suggestion," said Morgan.

The team sat down. Hannah slipped a pair of AA batteries into a plastic dome at the center of her game board. While she fidgeted with cards and playing pieces, Charles looked across the cafeteria and saw Keeley sitting at a table with all *his* teammates.

He remembered another one of his father's favorite *Art of War* quotes: "Victorious warriors win first and then go to war." Keeley talked big, but Charles suspected it wouldn't take much to knock him off his game before the afternoon auditions.

"Hannah?"

"Yes, Charles?"

"Are you good at that game?"

"She's the best," said Mirabai.

"Fascinating," said Charles. "I believe Kyle Keeley owns that same game."

"So?" said Hannah.

"Do you think you could defeat him?"

Hannah smiled. "I can beat anyone."

Charles came marching over to Kyle's cafeteria table.

He was followed by a girl carrying a board game box, as well as three other kids Kyle recognized as eighth graders.

"Hello," said the girl.

"Hey," said Kyle.

"I'm Hannah."

"Cool. I'm Kyle. These are my friends Akimi, Miguel, Sierra—"

"She knows who you people are!" snapped Charles.

"Even me?" said Andrew, sliding his glasses up the bridge of his nose. "Nobody ever knows who I am. I wasn't in the Lemoncello holiday commercials. You know why? Because I was kicked out of the escape game, thanks to you, Charles!"

"Ancient history," said Charles. "Hannah's on my *new* team. So are these other guys."

"You're Morgan Peden!" gushed Sierra. "You're my hero."

"Huh?" said Akimi.

"She's earned more Accelerated Reader points than any student who's ever attended AMS! She's also won every readathon since kindergarten!"

Morgan grinned. "Let's just say I've read a book or two."

"Big fan," said Sierra. "Big, big fan."

Meanwhile, Miguel was gawking at Ryan Capruso. "Weren't you the one who read all the Percy Jackson books in one weekend?"

"Yeah," said Ryan. "The next weekend, I read all the Harry Potters."

"And," said Charles, "Hannah and Mirabai here are co-captains of the eighth-grade BOB team."

Hannah placed the game board on the table and sat down directly across from Kyle. Charles and the others hovered behind her.

"So, I understand you've played this game before?" she said.

Mr. Lemoncello's Fantabulous Floating Emoji game was similar to charades, except the clues were given by 3-D graphics projected over the board by what the game box called a battery-powered "magic holographic eye."

"Yep," said Akimi, answering for Kyle. "Mr. Lemoncello gave us some of the very first copies."

"Cool. I'd like to challenge Kyle to a game."

"Okay," said Kyle. "But I have to warn you: We got our copies way before it even came out."

Hannah shrugged. "I don't care. I'll still beat you."

"Whooo!" said Miguel and Akimi.

"Feisty," added Andrew.

Kyle just nodded. "Game on," he said.

"Pick a disk," said Hannah, pointing to the stack piled up inside the lid of the game box.

"Go with 'famous children's books,'" said Charles. "Keeley won't know any. The only books his parents ever read to him when he was little were auto repair manuals. His old man is a grease monkey."

Kyle hated it when Charles made fun of his father. He reached for the "famous children's books" disk and slipped it into the projector.

"Famous kids' books it is," he said. "And you can go first, Hannah."

"I'll keep the time," said Miguel, fidgeting with his watch.

"Me too," said Charles.

"Fine," said Kyle, bopping the projector button. "Go!"

The first emoji floated over the game board.

45

"Next," said Hannah coolly.

Kyle tapped the button. A second emoji joined the first.

"*Alice's Adventures in Wonderland* by Lewis Carroll!" said Hannah.

The game's audio sensor detected a correct answer and exploded the emoji into a cloudburst of holographic confetti. After a tinny trumpet fanfare, the floating dots reformed to reveal the entire string of images that would've been available if Hannah had needed them.

"Ten seconds," said Miguel and Charles.

There was no dispute on the time.

Hannah was wicked fast.

"Good job," said Kyle.

"Thanks." She rotated the projector dome so the buttons were on her side. "Your turn. Ready?"

Kyle nodded. Hannah tapped the green button.
A fresh hologram floated over the game board.

Kyle looked at the emoji and said the first book title that popped into his head: *"Alexander and the Terrible, Horrible, No Good, Very Bad Day."*

"Wha-hut?" said Akimi.

"It's a boy. He could be Alexander. He looks like he's having a bad day. Next!"

Hannah hit the button. A second emoji joined the first.

Kyle stared hard at the floating images.

"Um, *Dead End in Norvelt* by, uh, that guy. You know. What's his name."

"Jack Gantos," said Sierra.

"This challenge is a one-on-one competition!" snapped Charles.

"Sorry."

"It's not the right answer, anyway," said Miguel. "Otherwise the emoji would've exploded."

"Next!" said Kyle.

Hannah pressed the button.

Nothing came up. The two floating emoji twinkled.

"That's it?" said Kyle. "No more clues?"

"Guess not," gloated Charles.

"Come on, Kyle," urged Miguel. "You've got this one, bro."

"No, he doesn't," said Charles.

"*Make Way for Ducklings*!" shouted Kyle. "*Creepy Carrots!* Uh, *Harry Potter and the Sorcerer's Road Sign.*"

"Er," said Akimi. "I don't see any ducks, carrots, or wizards. . . ."

"Because those answers are wrong, wrong, and wrong," said Charles. "By the way, you're at seventy seconds. That means you already lost a minute ago."

Kyle looked at Hannah. "Do you know it?"

She nodded.

"What's the answer?"

"*Where the Sidewalk Ends* by Shel Silverstein."

She wasn't just fast. She was also very, very good.

And Kyle?

He was very, very nervous.

12

How could Kyle go to game show tryouts in the auditorium at 3:10 when he was supposed to report to detention immediately after school at 3:05?

If he didn't show up in room 101, he'd earn two new detentions! Two more dreary days in a cinder-block room with nothing to do but homework. No games. No Wi-Fi. No nothing. And he could just imagine his parents' faces when they saw "SEVEN DETENTIONS" on his report card at the end of the term.

It would not be pretty.

But it will be worth it! Kyle decided.

No way was he missing out on a chance to star in Mr. Lemoncello's first-ever TV game show, live on Kidzapalooza.

"You ready?" Kyle said to Akimi when they met in the hallway after final period.

"Um, don't you have to go to—"

"The auditorium," Kyle said before she could utter the d-word. "That's where Mr. Lemoncello has set up shop, so that's where we need to be."

"Oh-kay," said Akimi. "But one of these days, we need to discuss 'making good choices.'"

"Sounds like fun. But not today."

Miguel, Sierra, and Andrew were waiting for Kyle and Akimi in the auditorium lobby. A dozen staff members from Mr. Lemoncello's Imagination Factory (they wore knit shirts with a lemon and a cello stitched where other shirts had polo ponies) sat smiling behind three long tables. The tables were lined with laptops and decorated with clumps of shimmering golden balloons. Kyle grinned. He'd hoped there might be balloons.

A mob of kids, maybe a hundred, broken down into five-member teams, was jostling forward, eager to get into the game.

"Yo," said Miguel, "each team has to pick its best code-cracker."

"Why?" asked Kyle.

"You have to beat the stupid computer," whined Andrew, "before you can even go into the auditions."

"Sadly," said Sierra, "they're doing their prescreening for gamers instead of readers."

"Because," Kyle said with a smile, "this is going to be a TV *game* show, not a TV *reading* show. But never fear, Kyle the game-meister is here. Let's do this thing!"

Kyle and his group joined a line and slowly made their way up to the table on the left.

"*Yes!*" screamed a team. They were in. Two more teams passed. Four teams failed. The passing teams received golden balloons. The failing teams got a box of lemon drops. Finally, Kyle and his friends made it to the front.

"Hi," said the chipper lady seated at the table. "Team name?"

"The Lemon Heads," said Akimi.

"We're the ones who won the escape game," added Kyle.

"Except me," said Andrew. "I was"—he did air quotes—"'disqualified.'"

"Sorry to hear it," said the lady. She typed the team name into her computer. "As you've probably heard, we're doing some preliminary testing out here. Trying to whittle down the contestant field." She swiveled the computer so Kyle and his friends could read the screen. "Here's your first puzzle. Kindly crack this code."

Kyle scanned the string of text:

**A P L R I O B C R E A E R D Y I I N S T A O B T O
H O E K A S U E D M I P T O O R R I I U U M M**

"We're dead," muttered Andrew.

"Read it backward," suggested Sierra. "Mr. Lemon-cello's done backward codes before."

Kyle shook his head. "This is different. Anybody got a pen and a piece of paper?"

"Yeah," said Andrew. "In my locker."

"You have two minutes," said the smiling lady seated behind the desk.

"It could be a substitution code," suggested Akimi. "Another one of those Caesar cipher deals . . ."

"Maybe," said Kyle.

"Maybe we need to shine an ultraviolet light on it!" said Andrew. "I saw that in a breakout game once. Who's got an ultraviolet flashlight?"

Miguel rolled his eyes. "Let me check my pockets."

"Wait, you guys," said Kyle. "I think it's a second-letters code. We need to write down every second letter. The first, the third, the fifth . . ."

"On it," said Akimi. She opened the notes app on her phone.

"When you finish, start again on the letters you skipped the first time through."

Akimi frantically thumbed the answer into her phone:

ALIBRARYISABOOKSEMPORIUM
PROCEEDINTOTHEAUDITORIUM

The rest of the team peered over her shoulders and broke the letters into words.

"A library is a books emporium," said Miguel.

"Proceed into the auditorium!" said everybody else.

"Well done!" said the lady behind the desk, tugging

on a tangle of curled ribbons to free a clump of five golden balloons, one for each member of the team. "The Lemon Heads can now, officially, audition for the show."

"Woo-hoo!" shouted Kyle. He and his friends slapped each other high fives very carefully because they didn't want to lose their balloons.

That was when Charles cried out, "Excellent! Good job, Ryan."

"It was a simple reversed-letters code," replied his teammate Ryan Capruso.

"Fine. Give us our golden balloons, please." Charles stuck out his hand. "But give me mine first. I'm the team captain. . . ."

"My friends," said Miguel, shaking his head in awe, "you're looking at a living legend. Ryan Capruso has checked out more library books than any other student in the history of Alexandriaville Middle School."

"No way," said Kyle.

"Way," said Sierra. "I hope my book log someday has as many titles in it as his does."

"Those four eighth graders?" said Miguel with great admiration. "They're this school's original Nerdy Book Club. And they are absolutely awesome."

Kyle felt his stomach tighten.

His archenemy was definitely in this breakout game to win it.

And with the all-star team of eighth graders he'd assembled, he just might be able to do it, too.

13

"Hearty and splendiferous greetings!" boomed Mr. Lemoncello from the auditorium stage. "If you made it into this auditorium, then you might be on your way to glorium!"

Mr. Lemoncello was decked out in a plaid sport coat, plaid pants, and plaid socks. His bow tie spun around like a whirling airplane propeller whenever he wiggled his ears. Except for his bright yellow banana shoes, he looked like an old-school TV game show host.

Dr. Zinchenko, dressed all in red as she always was, started randomly pointing to things. She reminded Kyle of that lady on *Wheel of Fortune*.

Six other teams had made it into the auditions with their golden balloons. Only two would advance to the televised game show at the library.

Kyle checked out the competition. There was Team Chiltington, of course. He also saw some other seventh graders who had formed two teams of their own, two more eighth-grade teams, and one team filled with eager sixth graders.

"I want to thank each and every one of you for being here today," said Mr. Lemoncello.

Then he said, "Thank you, thank you, thank *you*," thirty-five different times, once for every player seated in the auditorium. While he did, Dr. Zinchenko silently air-clapped—just like that lady who pointed at prizes on that other TV game show.

"Only two teams will advance to the All-Star Break-out Game, where you will become characters in fictional tales that take place inside the Fictionasium, a labyrinth of rooms conveniently located behind the fiction wall of my library—which, of course, is really *your* library, but there isn't room for all your names on the signage."

He took a deep breath.

"This afternoon, Dr. Zinchenko and I will lead you through a series of three quick games, each one cleverly designed to test your fictionary skills! The two teams with the highest scores will move on to the big TV game show! We will begin . . . right NOW!"

The first elimination round was, basically, a Battle of the Books competition with all sorts of questions about famous works of fiction.

"In which book does a boy grow a Padawan braid?"

"In which book does a character sit at a sea-green metal picnic table and eat ice cream?"

"In which book are two girls told to go to room four twenty-three and knock twice?"

Dr. Zinchenko asked the questions (dozens of them), and each team answered on an lPad (it was like an iPad but without the dot).

Thanks to Sierra, Andrew, Miguel, and Akimi (who knew the answers *Wonder, Counting by 7s, Sammy Keyes and the Hotel Thief,* and a bunch more), the Lemon Heads took second place in that round.

Charles and his team (they called themselves the Bookworms) came in first.

The second round was all about famous authors. And even though they were rebus puzzles projected on a screen, Kyle didn't know enough of the names to really help his team.

He gave up trying after the first three.

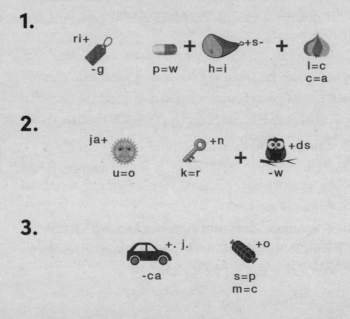

Fortunately, Dr. Zinchenko revealed the answers at the end of the round or Kyle never would've known who any of the authors were.

RITA WILLIAMS–GARCIA
JASON REYNOLDS
R. J. PALACIO

Surprising everyone, the team of sixth graders came in first.

Charles and his gang of eighth graders came in second.

Kyle and the Lemon Heads finished third.

"The stupid sixth graders beat us," groused Andrew.

"Which means they aren't stupid," said Akimi.

"This next and final game," announced Mr. Lemon-cello, "is my personal favorite. Because it puts you, the reader, in the middle of the action. Are you ready to begin your adventure?"

"Yes!" shouted all the kids in the auditorium.

Kyle shouted the loudest.

"Then on your mark, get set, Lemon, cello, go!"

Mr. Lemoncello aimed his remote at the screen.

A seemingly strange and scrunched-up sentence, typed in all caps, scrolled into view:

YOU ARE STANDING AT THE END OF A ROAD BEFORE A SMALL BRICK BUILDING. AROUND YOU IS A FOREST. A SMALL STREAM FLOWS OUT OF THE BUILDING AND DOWN A GULLY.

"As you type in your answer," boomed Mr. Lemoncello, "new options will appear on your lPads. Good luck!"

"What?" shouted Charles. "How can we enter an answer when you haven't even asked a question?"

Mr. Lemoncello just smiled and bobbed up and down on the heels of his banana shoes.

"East," Kyle whispered to Akimi, who had the team's lPad in her lap.

"Huh?"

"Type in the word 'east.'"

"Why?"

"Because it'll take us into the Colossal Cave!"

14

"East?" said Akimi. "Why?"

"Because," Kyle whispered, "Mr. Lemoncello took that line from the very first role-playing game ever designed for computers! It was all text and so primitive you could only type in one- or two-word commands."

"Here," said Akimi, passing the lPad to Kyle. "You take over."

Kyle had actually played the classic text-only game one summer when he was visiting his grandparents in Indiana. His grandpa had an antique Kaypro computer up in his attic (it was so old it used a pair of what his granddad called "floppy disks"). Since it was the only thing close to a video game at his grandparents' place, Kyle had spent two solid weeks exploring the sprawling nooks and crannies of Colossal Cave Adventure.

Now he maneuvered his way through the game's first rooms, picking up keys, food, and a shiny brass lamp.

"We'll need those when we get deeper into the cave," he told his friends. "We'll also need to battle an ogre to haul out the gold and treasure."

"Oh," said Andrew. "It's like that game with the dungeons and the dragons. I forget the name."

"Dungeons and Dragons," said Kyle.

"Oh. Right."

"You guys?" said Miguel. "Check it out. Everybody else is totally stumped."

Kyle picked up his playing pace. Because of their less-than-stellar showing in the first two games, he knew everything was riding on this one. After ten minutes, he had amassed a small fortune in treasure. Mr. Lemoncello called, "*Time!*" Then, to be fair, he called, "*National Geographic*!" and "*Sports Illustrated*!"

The lPads froze. Scores were electronically tallied.

"The results are in!" declared Mr. Lemoncello. "Adding the scores from this final round to the scores from the previous two, carrying the one, dividing by three, computing the average, not the mean, because nobody likes meanies . . ." He flickered his fingers in the air as if he were operating an invisible calculator. "Aha! The first team moving on is . . . the Bookworms."

"Yes!" shouted Charles. "I did it!"

"Dude?" said Ryan. "*We* did it."

His teammates shook their heads and rolled their eyes.

"The other team moving on . . . thanks in no small part to a stupendous surge in the third and final round . . . is the Lemon Heads!"

"Woo-hoo!" shouted Kyle and his four friends.

"It's us against Charles!" said Andrew. "Yes! I'm finally going to make him pay for knocking me out of the escape game."

"You should really let that go, Andrew," advised Sierra.

"Seriously, dude," added Miguel.

"Anger isn't healthy," said Akimi.

"But competition sure is!" added Kyle, with a wink to Andrew.

"Thanks to all of you for participating," said Mr. Lemoncello. "Those of you on the two winning teams will receive further instructions later this week. We will have an orientation for the game a week from Friday. Before then, you will be contacted by our costumers so you can be fitted for your motion capture suits. The game itself will take place a week from this Saturday at high noon. And for those of you who might be wondering: Yes, there will be balloons! Cake, too!"

15

All right! Kyle thought as he biked home. *Everything's going to work out!*

It was a Tuesday. The orientation was a week from Friday. Since he'd missed detention to go to the tryouts, he had six more left (four from the original five, plus the two penalty points). That was perfect. He had seven school days to serve them! Heck, he could even earn one more if he wanted to. Not that he wanted to. It was just good to have a buffer.

He leaned his bike against the garage door and bounded into his house. He and his friends were going to the Big Show! They were going to be on TV. And, more importantly, they were going to win!

Kyle's brothers were waiting for him the second he stepped through the front door. Mike was smirking like he knew something Kyle didn't.

"What?" said Kyle. "What's going on?"

"Heh, heh, heh" was all Mike said.

"Mom and Dad received an email," said Curtis.

"From who?"

"You mean 'whom.' "

"Okay, whom?"

"Charles Chiltington."

"What?" Kyle gasped. "Chiltington?"

"Kyle? Is that you?" It was his dad. In the kitchen.

"Get in here. Now." That was his mom.

"Hch, hch, hch," Mike chuckled again. "Good luck, Kyle. You're gonna need it."

Fearing the worst, Kyle made his way to the kitchen.

"Explain this," said his father.

His dad, still dressed in the green coveralls he wore to work, sat at the kitchen table, his fingers drumming a sheet of paper.

His mom sat there, too, shaking her head disappointedly.

"What exactly is it?" asked Kyle.

"An email," said his father. "From your friend Charles."

His father slid the sheet of paper across the table to Kyle.

Dear Mr. and Mrs. Keeley:

I hope this finds you both in excellent health and enjoying this fine day. Although it grieves me to be the bearer of ill tidings, I know that if I were a parent, charged with the wearisome burden of raising an irascible middle schooler, I would want to know the following: For his inappropriate actions at Alexandriaville Middle School, your son, Kyle James Keeley, was recently reprimanded with five detentions. I hope you don't mind my bringing this matter to your attention, but, as his friend, I thought it my duty, obligation, and responsibility to advise you that your son did not show up to serve detention this afternoon, thereby earning two additional detentions. I am worried that my chum Kyle might be spiraling out of control.

I look forward to seeing your well-manicured lawn and magnificent rosebushes again. Is Mrs. Keeley a professional horticulturist? It sure seems that way, judging by her excellent gardening skills.

> Concernedly,
> Your son's buddy and pal
> Charles Chiltington

Kyle looked up from the note. His ears were on fire.

How dare that slimy jerk do this to me?

He tried to smile for his parents.

"Well, you see—"

"Not now," said his father.

"But you asked me to explain—"

His dad pointed to the steps. "Go to your room, Kyle. You're grounded."

64

"B-b-but . . ."

"First you earn a detention and then you skip serving it?"

"W-w-well . . ."

"How many detentions did they give you?" asked his mother.

"Five," Kyle admitted with a sigh. "But since I missed one, I have six more. . . ."

"Six?" His dad nearly exploded. "Well, guess what? You're grounded for *two* weeks! And no games!"

"But, Dad—"

"We raised you better than this. Go to your room!"

"Yes, sir."

Kyle headed up the staircase.

When he reached the landing, he heard his mother say, "That Chiltington boy is so polite."

"Yeah," said his dad. "It's a shame Kyle can't be more like him."

Kyle closed his door and flopped down on his bed.

He still had his phone, so he texted Akimi.

> Bad news. Chiltington told my parents
> about the detentions. I'm grounded.

She wrote back immediately.

> How long?
>> Two weeks. I've never seen them this
>> mad. You need to find someone else for
>> the team.

> Hang in there. We'll think of something.
>
> > I hate Chiltington.
>
> So? Everybody hates Chiltington.
>
> > Not my parents. They wish I could be
> > more like him.
>
> Gag me now.

"Kyle?" It was his father, outside the bedroom door. "I hear keys clacking. Are you playing some kind of game?"

"No, sir."

Kyle quickly signed off with Akimi. And then, since his father had said he couldn't play a game, he did his homework.

But that only took an hour.

So, with nothing else to do, he picked up a book that Sierra Russell had lent him. It was one of her favorites. *The Watsons Go to Birmingham—1963* by Christopher Paul Curtis, the same author who wrote another one of Sierra's faves, *Bud, Not Buddy.*

All of a sudden, as the story carried him away, Kyle felt like he was Byron, the oldest son of an African American family in Flint, Michigan, way back in 1963. Byron gets in trouble, so his parents decide he should spend the summer, and maybe the next school year, with his grandmother down in Alabama. Kyle could relate. Especially since his parents were probably wondering if they should ship him off to his grandparents in Indiana for school next year.

Kyle wasn't an African American. He wasn't from

Flint, Michigan. He wasn't even born in 1963. But because the story was so good, while he read it he felt as if he were Byron. Maybe that was why Mr. Lemoncello always called fiction "the greatest role-playing game ever invented."

Around seven o'clock, someone knocked on his bedroom door.

"Come in," he said.

It was his dad. He had a ham sandwich with chips and a pickle on a plate.

"Remind me," he said. "How many detentions do you have left?"

"Six."

"And when's this live TV game show at the library?"

"Next Friday and Saturday. But how did you—"

"Akimi came over. Told us how you earned those detentions. How you accepted responsibility for your actions. How you protected your friends."

"Yes, sir."

His dad put the plate of food on Kyle's desk.

"She also told us a little bit more about the Chiltington boy. How he makes fun of you for what I do."

Kyle didn't know what to say.

"Okay, kiddo, here's the plan," said his dad. "You're going to serve those six detentions."

"Yes, sir."

"You're never, ever going to earn another one."

"No, sir."

"And then you are going to join Akimi, Andrew,

67

Miguel, and Sierra at the library for this new breakout game. Your friends need you."

"I'm ungrounded?"

"I don't think 'ungrounded' is a word."

"Yeah. Probably not."

"And, Kyle?"

"Yes, sir?"

"Go in there and make me proud!"

16

"Time for detention?" sneered Charles as Kyle made his way to room 101 after school.

"Yep," said Kyle cheerfully. "Last one."

"Did you see the Lemoncello breakout game countdown clock on Kidzapalooza last night?" Charles prodded. "The digital lemon?"

"I saw it, Charles. The whole world saw it."

"The game starts in less than seventy-two hours, Keeley. How unfortunate for you that you can't use the next hour to run fiction drills with your teammates, as I will be doing with mine."

"Doesn't matter how many drills you do, Charles. You're not going to win."

"Oh, really? And why is that?"

"Because my team is a real team. We're all working together. Nobody's in it for the gift cards."

"Those are merely performance incentives," said Charles defensively.

They rounded a corner. Akimi, Sierra, Miguel, and Andrew were all waiting outside room 101.

"We brought books," said Miguel.

"Some of our favorite works of fiction," added Andrew.

"Mine are marked with sticky notes," said Sierra.

"Some of mine are marked with sticky stuff, too," said Akimi. "Pizza cheese, caramel sauce, Twizzlers. I like to snack while I read."

"We'll silently read for an hour," said Miguel, "and then discuss what we've read after detention's done."

"Sounds like a plan," said Kyle. He and his friends headed into room 101.

"What?" Charles laughed. "You all have detentions?"

"Nope," said Kyle, jabbing a thumb over his shoulder. "But detention's a great place for reading. Soooo quiet . . ."

"B-b-but . . ."

Kyle shrugged. "It's what real teammates do, Charles. We stick together, no matter what. Just like the pages in Akimi's books."

The next day, Thursday, Kyle and his friends (along with Charles and his eighth-grade teammates) reported to the gym's locker rooms, where they were all fitted for their full-body MoCap suits by members of Mr. Lemoncello's staff.

"You guys look great," said the lead costumer.

"No," said Andrew, fidgeting with his snug gloves and headpiece, "we look like speed skaters who just got pelted with Ping-Pong balls."

"For you, Andrew," Charles said snidely, "that's a vast improvement."

"Take it easy, guys," said the costumer. "We know the MoCap suits look and feel weird at first. But on-screen, our computers will transform you into fully costumed characters."

"So cool!" said Kyle excitedly. "We're going to be the stars of an RPG!"

"Huh?" said Hannah Chung from Charles's team. "What's an RPG?"

"A role-playing game. You know—like Mr. Lemoncello's Quest of Cactus Island."

When everybody was back in their street clothes, the two teams were reminded to report to the Lemoncello library immediately after school the next day, Friday, for their orientation. The game itself would go on the air live at noon on Saturday.

Kyle was so excited, he had a hard time falling asleep Thursday night. Especially since the Kidzapalooza Network kept running nonstop promos for "*Mr. Lemoncello's All-Star Breakout Game*, featuring surprise guest stars— live this Saturday at noon!"

"You won't want to miss it, gang!" said Haley Daley as she ducked to dodge a flying pie. "Like that pie just missed me." Then a second pie fell, cream side down, from the ceiling and splattered on top of her head. Gloppy filling oozed down her face and she caught some with her tongue. "Okay. That's coconut cream. I still want chocolate!"

Kyle wondered who the guest stars might be. Haley? Jaylen Swell, the cool guy who always dabbed and dipped in a dance he called the Dip Dab? Maybe even Kai Kumar!

Focusing on schoolwork on Friday proved impossible, too. There were posters promoting the TV game show plastered up and down the halls. They promised "Big Surprises" and "Kidzapalooza-Sized Zaniness!" At lunch, it was all anybody kept talking about. During seventh period, there was even a pep rally in the gym filled with chants of "Readers are leaders!" and "Goooooo, fiction! Make stuff up!"

Seconds after the final bell, Kyle and his teammates bolted out of the building.

Everybody in the halls was screaming "Good luck!" and "You've got this!"

Except the eighth graders. They were all rooting for Charles's team.

Kyle's dad was waiting for the Lemon Heads in the school's pickup lane. He'd brought the tow truck. The one with room for five passengers.

"Tomorrow's the big day," Kyle's dad said as they drove through town, heading for the library. "You guys ready to rock?"

"Totally!" said Akimi.

"But first they have to explain the game to us," said Andrew.

"We can't win if we don't know the rules," added Kyle.

The tow truck rounded a bend, and everybody in it, including Kyle's father, said, "Whoa!"

There was a sea of bleachers set up in the town square in front of the domed library.

"That's where the live audience will watch the action," said Miguel. "Check out those giant TV screens!"

Each one was the size of a billboard. There were four of them lining the sides of the square.

Technicians aimed colorful spotlights at the library building's towering columns. Bunches of balloons were tied to sandbags. Purple and yellow bunting was being draped wherever the set decorators could find a place to drape it. Kyle noticed a booth on an elevated scaffold with two bright yellow director's chairs stationed in front of a pair of TV cameras.

"I bet that's where Mr. Lemoncello and Dr. Z will be doing the play-by-play and color commentary," said Akimi.

"And talking to the surprise guest stars!" added Kyle.

Mr. Keeley pulled to a stop. Kyle and his teammates tumbled out of the tow truck as quickly as they could.

"Have fun in there!" Kyle's dad called after them. "Text me when you're ready to be picked up."

"Thanks, Dad!"

Kyle and the rest of the Lemon Heads hurried up the

marble steps to the library's twenty-ton circular vault door. It was a holdover from when the building was the Gold Dome Bank. It was also unbelievably amazing.

Kyle paused and took a deep breath.

"You guys ready for this?"

"Uh, yeah," said Akimi. "This is just orientation, Kyle."

"Then let's go inside and get orientated!"

17

Nervous and excited at the same time, Kyle and his friends stepped through the dramatic doorway.

Charles Chiltington and his crew of eighth graders—the Bookworms—were already lurking in the lobby, standing right in front of the burbling statue of Mr. Lemoncello with his head tilted back so water could arc out of his mouth like he was winning a nonstop spitting contest.

"Well, look who made it," said Charles. "Doesn't your father need help rotating tires this weekend, Keeley?"

"Nope," said Kyle. "He needs me to beat you."

"Ha! In your dreams. As *my* father reminded me moments ago, 'Chiltingtons never lose.'"

"Well then," cracked Akimi, "he must be totally disappointed in you."

Kyle saw Charles wince, if only for a second.

"Pay no attention to these simpering seventh graders,"

Charles told his teammates. "I guarantee that we shall win. Kyle Keeley and his unfortunate associates shall whine!"

"Yeah, right, Charles," said Akimi. "Like that's ever going to happen. Come on, you guys."

Kyle's team hurried through the arched hallway that led into the cavernous Rotunda Reading Room. Half of the circular room was filled with three-story-tall bookshelves—Mr. Lemoncello's famous fiction wall.

Overhead, the ten wedge-shaped ultrahigh-definition screens of the rotunda's Wonder Dome were swirling with a flurry of famous book covers. *Wonder. The Jumbies. The Epic Fail of Arturo Zamora. The Stars Beneath Our Feet. Peter Nimble and His Fantastic Eyes. A Snicker of Magic. Three Times Lucky. Bad Magic. The Island of Dr. Libris.*

"They're all fiction titles," said Miguel.

"And they keep changing," added Andrew, staring up at the iridescent ceiling. "It's making me dizzy."

"So quit staring at it," advised Miguel.

"I can't! It's mesmerizing."

"The statues under the dome keep changing, too," said Sierra, pointing to the arched niches arrayed around the room. Holograms glowing a ghostly green faded in and out of view. "There's Albus Dumbledore. Charlotte from *Charlotte's Web*. Encyclopedia Brown. Peter from *The Snowy Day*. Eloise. Junie B. Jones. None of them are real, but I feel like I know them all!"

"Welcome, welcome, welcome!"

Mr. Lemoncello appeared on the second-floor balcony. He was costumed in a beret, a hip-length safari jacket, billowy riding pants, and shiny black boots. He spoke through a megaphone and looked like a Hollywood movie director from the 1930s.

"Will both middle school teams kindly join us in the Rotunda Reading Room?" he called through the megaphone.

Charles Chiltington and his team of geniuses scurried in from the lobby.

Mr. Lemoncello scampered down a spiral staircase. His banana shoes burp-squeaked "Hooray for Hollywood" the whole way. Dr. Zinchenko, dressed in a glamorous red-sequined gown, gracefully sashayed behind him.

"As you may have noticed," said Mr. Lemoncello, "we have temporarily removed the hover ladders from in front of the fiction shelves. They are currently at my house, where I am using them to wash my hard-to-reach windows, attack cobwebs, and change a few lightbulbs."

"But," said Dr. Zinchenko, "that is not why the ladders were removed. We needed them out of the way so that we might add windows, doors, and mirrors to the fiction wall."

She gestured toward the three-story-tall bookcases.

Kyle didn't see any windows, doors, *or* mirrors.

He raised his hand.

"Yes, Kyle?" said Dr. Z.

"I don't see them."

"Me neither," said Charles.

"Ah!" said Mr. Lemoncello, slapping his forehead. "My mistake. We forgot to hand out these!"

He reached into the hip pockets on both sides of his baggy jodhpur pants and pulled out a stack of extremely thin smartphones.

"There's one for each of you," he said. "You are not to use them for texting, Instagramming, tweeting, or ordering pizza. But they *are* equipped with the augmented-reality app you will need to play this game!"

Mr. Lemoncello and Dr. Zinchenko passed out the phones.

Kyle held his up.

Suddenly, on the screen, floating in front of the bookshelves, he saw windows, doors, and mirrors.

"This is just like that game Lemoncello Go," Miguel whispered to Kyle, "where you go around town capturing monsters in your phone."

"I loved that game!" said Kyle.

"Who's ready to go someplace they've never been before?" asked Mr. Lemoncello, his eyes twinkling. "Who's ready to be someone they've never been before? Who's ready to say 'Hello, Universe' or travel the long way down? Who would like to be the girl who drank the moon?"

Every one of the players shot up their hands.

"Well then—welcome to the fantabulous world of fiction!"

18

Holding up their new phones, the ten contestants followed Mr. Lemoncello and Dr. Zinchenko over to the fiction bookcases, marveling at the floating 3-D images of brightly colored windows, doors, and mirrors that had magically appeared on their screens.

"Mr. Chiltington?" said Mr. Lemoncello.

"Yeah?"

"Go ahead. Open any door you like."

"But they're not real. They don't really exist."

"Ah, but this is the fiction wall. All sorts of things you think can't exist suddenly do!"

"I'll try it," said Kyle, reaching out and grabbing what looked like a door handle created by the spine of a book jutting out just a few inches farther on the shelf than all the others. "Hey! This part is real."

Kyle tugged. A door-sized panel of books swung open.

"Cool!"

"I'm doing this mirror!" shouted Charles, pulling on the spine of another book poking out from the shelf. Three rows of books slid to the side like the mirror on a medicine chest.

Both teams crowded behind their captains and peered through the openings in the bookcase.

"There's nothing inside ours," whined Andrew. "It's just a gaping black void!"

"This is so lame," said Charles.

"There's nothing there now," said Mr. Lemoncello. "But tomorrow at noon, when the game officially begins, these windows, doors, and mirrors will lead you into the Fictionasium!"

"What's that?" asked Sierra.

"Behind this wall," boomed Mr. Lemoncello, gesturing grandly, "is a labyrinth of rooms where stories come to life—and *you* become their main characters. In each scenario, you will be presented with a puzzle. Solve it, and you will break out of that room with a key that will unlock one of the five locks on your codex!"

"Our what?" said Charles.

"An ancient manuscript text in book form," said his teammate Morgan Peden.

"From the Latin word *codex,* for 'block of wood,'" added Ryan Capruso.

"Later denoting a block split into leaves or tablets for writing on," said Mirabai Keshap.

"Hence a book," finished Hannah Chung.

"Correctomundo, Bookworms!" crowed Mr. Lemoncello. "Well done and well defined!"

Kyle looked at his teammates. They all had the same semi-sick, semi-panicked look on their faces. Charles's team was better than good. They were awesome.

Beaming, Charles bounced up and down on his toes. "We are *so* going to win this thing!"

Mr. Lemoncello raised his megaphone to his lips. "Clarence? Kindly roll in the codexes!"

"Or codices," said Mirabai. "Both plurals are acceptable."

The burly security guard, his dreadlocks swinging, pushed a library cart into the room. Two leather-bound books, each the size of a stack of laptops, were propped on the cart's slanted top shelf. Each thick, antique cover was held in place by elaborate brass hinges and shackled shut with an equally ornate clasp. Five brightly colored and differently shaped locks dangled from each hasp's hoop.

"Five different locks," said Mr. Lemoncello. "For five different rooms."

"Each lock color," said Dr. Zinchenko, "corresponds to a genre of fiction. Each codex is sealed with a different collection of locks. Each team will need to explore its own path through the Fictionasium in order to break out of the library."

"We will pick the genres for you," explained Mr. Lemoncello. "Because some of you need windows more

81

than doors. Others, mirrors more than windows. And all of us need to read without walls!"

"What's he talking about?" mumbled Akimi. "Are we going camping?"

Kyle shrugged. Sometimes Mr. Lemoncello confused him, too. He didn't always know where Mr. Lemoncello's games were going, but he always enjoyed the ride.

"Can we cut to the chase?" demanded Charles. "How do we win?"

"Unlock all five locks on your codex," said Mr. Lemoncello. "Inside, you will find a secret surprise! Something that will help you unlock one final lock: the one securing the library's front door from the inside. The first team to unlock that lock and break out of the library will be declared the winners."

"And star in their very own TV game show on Kidzapalooza!" shouted Kyle. "Woo-hoo!"

"Now, remember," said Dr. Zinchenko, "you will only have two hours to work your way through all five of your genre-specific stories and break out of the library."

"Five locks in two hours?" said Miguel. "No problemo."

"You will also need to avoid treacherous tricks and other devious devices."

"It wouldn't be a game without a few devious devices and treacherous tricks, now would it?" said Mr. Lemoncello proudly.

Kyle heard Sierra gulp. She never really liked the treacherous and tricky stuff.

"Since this is a TV game show," Dr. Zinchenko continued, "everything you do will be captured by cameras located in each of the Fictionasium rooms. All of your actions will be broadcast for millions to see."

"The whole world will be watching," said Mr. Lemoncello. "Therefore, I hope your journeys will be as miraculous as Edward Tulane's!"

"Who's he?" Kyle whispered to Akimi.

"You really need to read more books, Kyle," Akimi whispered back.

Morgan asked the next question: "Will our stories be based on famous books, such as *The Miraculous Journey of Edward Tulane* by Kate DiCamillo, which was originally published in 2006 by Candlewick Press and went on to win the Boston Globe–Horn Book Award for fiction?"

Mr. Lemoncello smiled. "Would you mind if I gave your forty-three-word question a one-word answer?"

"Of course not."

"Good. No. Oh, my. That was *two* one-word answers. The premise, supporting players, and settings for your stories—be they horror, science fiction, fantasy, mystery, or realistic fiction—shall be made up by me, your story master, with the aid and assistance of the Narrative Drive supercomputer. You, the players, will dictate the plots of your stories based on how you interact with the characters and settings you encounter in each room."

"This has to be the coolest role-playing game ever invented!" gushed Kyle.

"No, Kyle," said Mr. Lemoncello. "That would be an actual book! Now then, please report back here tomorrow, no later than ten a.m., when our third team will have arrived."

"What?" said Kyle. "There's a third team?"

"Yo," said Miguel. "It's a plot twist, bro. This is fiction. Get used to them."

19

"Guys?" Kyle called to his brothers. "Hurry up! We don't want to be late!"

"It's not even nine o'clock," yawned a sleepy-eyed Mike, who was buttering his toast in slow motion. "Besides, it's a Saturday."

"But I have to be at the library at ten," said Kyle. "Traffic could be bad. They're expecting thousands of spectators in the stands."

"I suggest we all pack pillows and/or seat cushions," added Curtis. "Aluminum bleachers can numb one's gluteus maximus."

"You mean our butts?" asked Mike.

Curtis nodded and cut the crusts off his toast. Also in slow motion.

"Tell you what, Kyle," said his dad. "Why don't I drive you down to the library now? Mom can bring Mike and

Curtis in her car when everybody's finished with breakfast."

"But what will you do?" Kyle asked his dad. "The game doesn't start till noon."

"I'll make sure the Keeley family has the best seats in the house. Come on, Kyle. Let's hit the bricks."

On the drive downtown, the butterflies in Kyle's stomach had butterflies in *their* stomachs. He'd never been so excited. Or nervous. Charles's team was good. And now there would be a third team? Two teams would be harder to defeat than just one.

". . . proud of you."

Oops. Kyle's father was talking to him, but Kyle had crawled too deep inside his own thoughts to hear what his dad was saying.

"Huh?" he said.

"Win, lose, or draw," his father said, probably repeating himself, "I'm proud of you, Kyle. And remember: Sometimes you learn more from losing than you do from winning. When you lose, you learn how to keep going."

"Um, you want me to lose?"

"No. I want you to go inside and have fun. Because that's what games are supposed to be. Fun."

"Right. Thanks!"

Kyle stepped out of the truck. His dad drove off to find a parking spot.

Everywhere Kyle looked, he saw bustling TV crew people. Some were laying cable, others aiming extremely bright lights. It also looked like they'd already inflated every balloon in the state of Ohio. Four semitrailers with attached staircases served as portable control rooms for the live broadcast. Another trailer was labeled "Hair and Makeup."

A woman with a clipboard saw Kyle gawking at everything and called out his name.

"Kyle Keeley?"

"Yes, ma'am?"

"You're early."

"Yeah. Kind of."

"Report to the wardrobe trailer. You need to put on your MoCap suit."

"Is the other team here?"

"Which one? The Bookworms or the All-Stars?"

"The All-Stars?" said Kyle.

"Our special surprise guests. Five stars from your favorite Kidzapalooza shows."

"Seriously?"

"The celebs are inside the library with Dr. Z," said the lady, checking her watch. "Go in and say hello. You've got time."

"Thanks!"

Kyle jogged up the steps two at a time and passed through the bank vault door, which, of course, would be locked and sealed once the breakout game started.

Clarence, the burly security guard, and his equally burly twin brother, Clement, stood like a seven-foot-tall brick wall, blockading the entrance to the Rotunda Reading Room.

"Uh, hi, guys," said Kyle.

"Hey, Kyle," said Clarence. "You're not with the paparazzi, right?"

"No, sir."

Clarence and his brother both stepped aside. "Then you may enter. And guess what?"

"What?"

"Haley Daley's back in town!"

Kyle hurried into the Rotunda Reading Room.

He could see the back of Haley's head near the fiction wall, where Dr. Zinchenko had just finished explaining the whole windows-doors-mirrors augmented-reality-app thing to the new team.

"Cooltastic," said Jaylen Swell, raising both arms to strike a dab pose. He also flossed a little. Kyle recognized Jaylen and his signature moves from his Kidzapalooza dance and stunt show *I Double Dab Dare You*.

"You five should report to wardrobe," said Dr. Zinchenko. "If you will excuse me, I must consult with Mr. Lemoncello and Mr. Raymo. Apparently, the lightning-bolt blaster in the Mythology Room is acting up."

Dr. Zinchenko clicked away on her red high-heeled shoes.

Acting as nonchalant as he could, Kyle strode over to

where Haley and her TV star teammates were hanging out. His heart was racing. He had never met even one Kidzapalooza celeb before. Haley Daley was just, you know, *Haley Daley* back when she lived in Alexandriaville.

Haley saw Kyle approaching.

"Hey, hey, Kyle!" she squealed. "Ohmigosh. I haven't seen you since, what? Forever? Or longer. What's longer than forever?"

Then Haley totally shocked Kyle. She threw her arms around his neck and gave him a ginormous hug. She smelled like a bubble-gum-scented bubble bath.

"You guys?" Haley said to the other Kidzapalooza players. "This is Kyle Keeley."

"Oh, yeah," said Jaylen. "You were in those holiday commercials that made Haley, like, totally blow up."

"Thanks, Jaylen," said Haley with a giggle. "You're super sweet to say that." She giggled again and her giggle sounded gigglier than Kyle remembered it. Haley's hair was blonder, too. Like it had gold flakes painted into it.

"So," she told Kyle, "as you know, this is Jaylen Swell, star of *I Double Dab Dare You*. And this goofy guy, who I, like, totally *adore*, is Kai Kumar."

"From *Sludge Dodgers*!" said Kyle. "Awesome show! You're hysterical in it."

"Thank you, my friend," said Kai. Leaning in to shake Kyle's hand, he pretended to slip on a banana peel. "Yikes!" He flipped up both his feet and landed on his butt.

"Funny!" gushed Haley. "Am I right? Fun-knee!"

Kai popped back up, unfazed.

"I wear padded underpants," he said. "Buy 'em in bulk."

"Next to Kai," said Haley, "is Gabrielle Grande."

"From *Blam-a-Wham-a-Rama*," said Kyle, recognizing Kidzapalooza's biggest and probably oldest star.

"Gabby sings way better than I do!" said Haley.

"Do not!" giggled Gabrielle.

"Do too," Haley giggled back.

"Not!"

"Too!"

A buff kid who also looked to be fifteen or sixteen—and even more jock-ish than Kyle's big brother Mike—stepped forward to shake Kyle's hand. He had a grip like a vise.

"I'm Peyton McCallister," he said. "From *Maximum Me*."

"The extreme sports show!" said Kyle. He loved *Maximum Me*, especially the bike stunts. Peyton had muscles everywhere superheroes had them, plus a dimple in the middle of his chin. "Catch me at my max, Mondays at seven, six Central."

"Who's on *your* team?" Haley asked Kyle.

"Akimi, Miguel, Sierra, and Andrew."

"The gang from Alexandriaville Middle School? Awesome sauce! What about Charles Chiltington?"

"He's the captain of the other team."

"Seriously?" said Haley. "They're letting him play after how he cheated in the first game?"

Kyle shrugged. "I don't write the rules."

"Who'd he con into playing with him?"

"Some very smart eighth graders. They'll be here at ten. I'm kind of early."

"Cool."

Peyton flicked a finger back and forth between Gabrielle Grande and himself.

"We're a thing," he said. "Romantic to the max! Read about us in *Tiger Beat*."

"Follow us on Instagram," added Gabrielle.

Kyle nodded. "I'll do that. After the game."

"Nervous, kid?" asked Peyton.

"Little bit."

"You should be. If you've ever seen *Maximum Me*, you know I'm competitive to the max. That's not just my show's slogan. That's my brand."

"Dude?" said Jaylen, who had a slow and easy drawl. "We're all supercompetitive."

"I guess that's why we're All-Stars," said Gabrielle with a stunning smile, which she immediately switched off so she could give Kyle the stink-eye. "And you're not."

Kyle tried to smile.

But deep down, he wondered if the two teams from the local middle school were like the team of unlucky stooges who always played against the undefeated Harlem Globetrotters.

Maybe that was why Mr. Lemoncello hadn't held nationwide auditions.

Maybe the locals were only in the game to lose and make the Hollywood stars seem even more spectacular.

20

"Is everyone ready?" asked the stage manager, the lady with the clipboard. "We're live in thirty minutes!"

Excitement was definitely in the air. Balloons, too. Haley watched a monitor showing the crowd of people packed into the bleachers outside the library in the town square. She could see Kyle Keeley's whole family in the front row.

Haley's family was at their new home in California. Even though she was now a star and could afford to fly them all to Ohio, she had to be prudent with her finances. Stardom never lasted forever. Besides, her father wasn't all that interested in heading back to Alexandriaville.

On the nearest monitor, Haley watched Kai Kumar, the slapstick comedian who starred in *Sludge Dodgers*, warm up the crowd outside with a series of rapid-fire jokes and pratfalls.

"When you see the applause sign, clap. When you see the applesauce sign, duck!"

Right on cue, gallons of chunky applesauce tumbled out of a giant vat and slimed Kai.

The crowd loved it.

"Guess I better go inside and get cleaned up!" said Kai, after someone tossed him a bright purple Kidzapalooza beach towel. "The game is about to begin."

The audience cheered wildly. Kai waved and dashed through the library's bank vault front door. The guy was a pro. He'd taught Haley a lot. About comedy, timing, and managing her money.

Once Kai was back inside the building with all the other contestants, Mr. Lemoncello stepped out to greet the crowd.

He swung open his arms. "Is this going to be fun?"

Five thousand people replied, "Hello? It's a Lemon-cello!"

"Yes!" shouted Mr. Lemoncello. "I am!"

He bowed and made a grand show of locking and sealing the library's heavy front door by twirling its shiny copper spindle—a wheel that looked like it could steer a steamship.

"Henceforth and forthwith," Mr. Lemoncello declared, "the only contestants coming out of this enormous door shall be the ones who, somehow, successfully break out of the library and win today's game!"

The crowd roared some more.

"I myself," proclaimed Mr. Lemoncello, "shall be going in and coming back out before that happens—through a secret tunnel! Dr. Zinchenko and I will be hosting today's game from our perch here on the porch. I shall be back in, oh, thirty minutes. Until then, kindly keep my perch warm."

He pulled a slippery fish fillet out of his topcoat and tossed it to a production assistant.

Inside the Rotunda Reading Room, all the white-hot lights made it feel like the earth suddenly had three suns. Haley had grown used to all the lights, cameras, and action of Hollywood. But it looked like Kyle and her friends from Alexandriaville were sweating inside their tight-fitting MoCap suits. Charles Chiltington's team was wearing the Ping-Pong-ball-dotted unitards, too. They looked particularly miserable.

Haley Daley and the rest of the Kidzapalooza All-Stars weren't wearing the motion capture outfits. They were dressed the way they typically dressed on their TV shows.

Kai Kumar, who had quick-changed into a dry T-shirt and jeans (the same clothes he always wore on *Sludge Dodgers*), came bounding in from his gig warming up the crowd outside the library.

"How's my hair?" he asked a makeup artist. "Do I have apple chunks in it?"

"No more than usual," joked Gabrielle Grande.

"Cute, Gabby. Cute."

Haley had loved Gabrielle Grande's show ever since she was in first grade. Gabrielle was a much bigger star at Kidzapalooza than Haley. Had been for years. But lately, Haley'd heard whispers (behind Gabrielle's back, of course) that her time was "nearly up" and that Haley was "coming on strong."

One thing Haley learned quickly? Hollywood would always be way more competitive than any game Mr. Lemoncello could ever dream up.

A makeup person brushed Kai's hair clean and gooshed it so it looked neatly messy.

Haley glanced over at Charles Chiltington. She remembered how he'd tried to bully her during the escape game. She also remembered (quite fondly) how she'd outsmarted him.

Charles did a little finger-wiggle wave at her. "Hello, Haley."

"Hey, Charles. Great to see you again."

"Ditto. I know I speak for all of Alexandriaville when I say it is quite an honor, privilege, and joy to welcome you home."

"Um, thanks."

"And should your career in Hollywood falter, as, I fear, most do, we would be happy to have you and your family return to Ohio. My father could, most likely, help your father find work. I take it he's still out of a job and you're the family's primary breadwinner?"

Haley kept smiling. It took a great deal of effort, but

she couldn't let Charles push her buttons. She was an actress. She could pretend his words didn't get to her. Plus, she was Haley Daley, star of *Hey, Hey, Haley,* not a secretly insecure cheerleader from the wrong side of town who everyone thought was a ditzy airhead. At least not anymore.

"Oh, snap, Hales," said Gabrielle. "Who's the rude dude with the bad 'tude?"

"Meet Charles Chiltington," said Haley, laughing as if the insults were no biggie. "The biggest loser from the escape game."

"I wasn't the *only* loser," said Charles.

"True," said Andrew, raising his hand. "But during the Library Olympics, I became a winner!"

"You guys?" said Sierra Russell. Haley remembered her as a timid bookworm. "Let it go. That's ancient history."

"Typically found in the nine-zero-nine section of a library categorized according to the Dewey decimal system," said Mirabai Keshap from Charles's team.

"I don't care about all those other silly Lemoncello games!" snapped Charles. "This is the only one anyone will remember! This one will be on TV!"

"Charles?" said Hannah. "Have you ever considered yoga or meditation? You have serious anger management issues. . . ."

"Makeup?" shouted Peyton McCallister, jutting out his chest and chin. "Charles over here needs a touch-up. His face is turning pink. No, wait. Purple."

The Kidzapalooza gang laughed.

Charles glared at Peyton. "He who laughs last laughs loudest, Mr. McCallister."

"No," said Jaylen Swell. "He who laughs last usually just didn't get the joke."

"Contestants?" called Dr. Zinchenko. She click-clacked into the room on her high heels, dressed in her jazziest red dress ever. "Kindly join me here at the fiction wall. It's time to pass out your GOOHFER cards."

"GOOHFER cards?" Miguel wondered out loud.

Kyle grinned. "Guess it's just another one of those plot twists, bro."

21

"Everyone, settle down, please," said Dr. Zinchenko as the fifteen contestants clustered around her in front of the fiction wall. "Mr. Lemoncello would like to say a few words to you before the game begins."

"Um, where is he?" asked Kyle.

Suddenly, a floor panel popped open and Mr. Lemoncello shot out of it with a *WHOOSH* and a line of puffy white smoke trailing behind him.

"Woo-hoo!" he cried as he flew ten, fifteen, twenty feet above the floor. He had to hang on to his top hat to keep it from flying off. At the peak of his ascent, Mr. Lemoncello popped open his sturdy yellow umbrella. Using it like a handheld parachute, he gently drifted down, Mary Poppins–style, to the floor. "And that, boys and girls, is what it's like to be shot out of the world's largest T-shirt cannon!"

"Do we get to try it?" shouted Kyle.

Mr. Lemoncello winked at him. "Maybe later. After the show?"

"Cool!"

"Is everything as it should be down below?" asked Dr. Zinchenko.

"Yes," said Mr. Lemoncello. "The front door has been secured, so I came in through the backdoor sideways emergency exit."

"Fourteen minutes!" shouted the lady with a clipboard. She also had a stopwatch.

"Then, like Castle 'Ghost' Crenshaw, we better make this speedy!" said Mr. Lemoncello. He gestured at a waist-high console that reminded Kyle of a miniature ATM on a swivel arm. "Dr. Zinchenko? Kindly explain how that thingamabob-a-gizmo-a-jig works."

"With these cards," said Dr. Zinchenko. She handed out shiny plastic rectangles, each one a little larger than a playing card, to all the players. The cards sparkled and featured a moving image of each player. Kyle's avatar even waved up at him.

"These are your 'Get Out of Here Free Emergency Rescue,' or GOOHFER, cards. If at any time the game becomes too intense, too real, or too scary, simply slide your card into one of the control boxes located throughout all the rooms of the Fictionasium. Once you do, you will drop out of the game."

"Literally," said Mr. Lemoncello. "You'll fall down to the basement, where you will be rolled out to the emergency exit by the swelling sea of our undulating inflatable floor. It's very safe. Like being in a bouncy house or surfing on a wave of whoopee cushions."

"Once you drop out of the game," said Dr. Zinchenko, "your team may continue on its quest without you, penalty-free."

"Ha!" laughed Charles. "None of us will be quitting. Quitters never win and winners never quit."

A camera swooped down on a boom crane.

"We need to line up the first shot, Mr. L," said the lady with the clipboard.

Mr. Lemoncello smiled and looked directly into the lens.

"Oh, dear," he said, checking his reflection in the glass and picking at his teeth. "I suppose kettle corn wasn't a wise choice for breakfast this morning."

"Is everybody ready to play?" asked Dr. Zinchenko.

"To the max!" said Peyton.

"You are so awesome," said Gabrielle, patting one of his thick biceps.

"Being awesome is what I do, babe."

"Is grossing people out something else you do?" Akimi muttered out of the side of her mouth.

"We're live in three minutes!" shouted the clipboard lady.

Kyle looked at the monitor showing the huge audience in the town square. His whole family was in the front row. They'd made "Go, Lemon Heads" signs and everything.

The three teams were shown where to stand. Behind Mr. Lemoncello. In front of the fiction wall.

Spotlight beams started swinging back and forth across the rotunda. The Wonder Dome became a kaleidoscopic prism of geometric shapes and colors. The TV crew grew eerily quiet. The only thing Kyle could hear was his heart thumping in his chest.

"Hey, Kyle?" said Haley, because they were standing pretty close to each other.

"Yeah?"

"Good luck."

"Thanks. You too."

The lady with the clipboard started her final countdown.

"Okay, people. We're live in five, four, three, two . . ."

She pointed at Mr. Lemoncello.

The game was on!

22

Nobody said anything.

Kyle could hear the lady's stopwatch ticking.

Finally, three long seconds later, Mr. Lemoncello exploded into the camera lens.

"Hell-o! I'm a Lemon-cell-o! Welcome, one and all, to the first of my Never-Bored Board Games, right here on Kidzapalooza—where kids rule! Today, these three intrepid teams will be writing their own stories inside my revolutionary new Fictionasium as they try to break out of my library!"

The audience applauded.

Mr. Lemoncello turned and gestured toward the fiction wall.

"Hidden behind this great wall—which is far greater than the one in China because this one is built of books, not bricks—are rooms where amazing stories will spring to life. Jimmy? Who do we have playing with us today?"

"Well, Mr. Lemoncello," boomed an off-screen voice, "from your hometown of Alexandriaville, Ohio . . ."

"Go, Buckeyes," said Mr. Lemoncello.

". . . we have two teams of magnificent middle schoolers. They'll be going up against . . . the Kidzapalooza All-Stars!"

While Jimmy, the smooth-as-melting-butter announcer, crooned through the names of all the local contestants, the live feed cut to iconic images of the players superimposed over the cheering crowd out in the town square.

When Kyle's name was announced, his whole family leapt to their feet to give him a standing ovation.

"And from your favorite Kidzapalooza shows," Jimmy continued, "please welcome a glittering galaxy of glamorous all-stars!"

The Kidzapalooza celebrities were introduced with quick clips from their TV shows.

"Funnyman Kai Kumar! Sensational songstress Gabrielle 'Gabby' Grande! Newcomer Haley Daley! The cooltastic dabbing dude himself, Jaylen Swell. And, of course, the dashing and daring Peyton McCallister!"

Peyton raised his fist and shouted, "To the max!"

The crowd outside went wild.

"Thank you, Jimmy," said Mr. Lemoncello. "We've met the players. Now let's bring out their playing pieces!"

Clarence, his twin brother, Clement, and Dr. Zinchenko

ceremoniously wheeled in a library cart carrying three locked codexes.

A camera operator with a handheld unit moved in to cover the action as Dr. Zinchenko presented each team captain with their elaborately decorated locked book.

Hands trembling slightly, Kyle examined his team's codex.

There were five locks clamped through its brass hasp: red, blue, yellow, purple, green. Each lock was different. The red one was a classic combination wheel, like you'd use on your school locker. Blue was a three-digit lock—the kind some people have on suitcase zippers. Yellow needed a key. Purple didn't have numbers or letters, just a knob you could push up and down or side to side. Green was a lock with five rotating letter wheels.

"To break out of the library, you must first unlock all five locks on your codex," said Mr. Lemoncello. "Inside, you will find something that will help you unlock the lock on the library's front door! And believe me, that last lock is a lock-mess monster! For the next two hours, no one on the outside will be able to open it. Only someone inside."

"Surely you have a master key," said Jaylen.

"No, Jaylen, I don't. And please—don't call me Shirley. Dr. Zinchenko, Clement, this camera crew, and I will now exit the building the way you will if you decide to call it quits: through the floor! Once you are inside the Fiction-asium, dozens of remote-controlled cameras will cover all the action."

"What about Clarence?" asked Kyle. He was worried about his friend being left behind.

"Aha! Clarence will be in the control room with the Narrative Drive supercomputer, making sure everything hums along smoothly. Now then, I know we're all Edward Eager to get started, because what will happen inside the Fictionasium's story rooms is half magic, half high-tech, and one hundred percent amazible. So, who's ready to play *Mr. Lemoncello's All-Star Breakout Game* and win their own Never-Bored Board Game show on the Kidzapalooza Network?"

All fifteen players cheered enthusiastically.

"Very well," said Mr. Lemoncello. "Phones up, boys and girls."

Kyle raised his smartphone, which was already running the augmented-reality app. He was looking for a window, a door, or a mirror but couldn't see any.

"Are you ready to go places you've never been before?" asked Mr. Lemoncello. "Are you ready to become people you've never been before? Are you ready to break out of your comfort zones and break out of this library?"

"I'm ready to win!" shouted Charles.

"Then on your mark! Get set! Lemon, cello, go!"

23

The AR viewers simultaneously sprang to life.

Kyle could see a flashing red door on the wall of books. He also saw a pink mirror and an orange window.

"We need red!" Kyle shouted. "For our red lock. We don't need pink or orange."

"Hurry!" cried Andrew. "Chiltington's team already opened their pink mirror, and Haley's crew is sliding open an orange window!"

"Got it," said Akimi, who was the closest to the red door. She grabbed its knob and yanked it open.

The rest of the team followed her through the door and into the darkness beyond. When they were all in and Kyle pulled the door shut, the walls of the tunnel lit up in a rainbow of colors. It was like being inside a roll of assorted-flavor Life Savers.

"Welcome, LEMON HEADS," purred a soothing voice

from the ceiling speakers. "Some books are doorways into worlds we have never imagined. Your first genre is . . ."

The curving glass windows in the tubular corridor clicked through a range of colors until they all glowed red.

"Comic books."

"Comic books?" said Sierra. "That's not a genre. I'd understand if they said 'graphic novels.' But comic books?"

"Come on, you guys," said Kyle. "We have five locks and less than two hours. Something in here has to help us open the red lock on our codex."

"You are correct, LEMON HEADS," said the voice in the ceiling. "Please name someone or something you would see on a suburban street first thing in the morning."

"The garbageman," said Andrew.

"The newspaperboy," said Kyle.

"SIERRA?" asked the voice.

"I don't know. A dog with her walker?"

"Very well," said the voice. "Proceed into your first story. And good luck breaking out of the library!"

"You guys?" said Akimi, who'd gone on a scouting mission up the human gerbil tube of a hallway. "There's another door up ahead. And it looks just like the cover to a Marvel comic book!"

Kyle and the others followed Akimi back up the hall and stared at the glowing door.

"Okay," said Akimi. "It's different now."

A title was splashed across the top of the door in bold comic-book lettering:

GARBAGEMAN! SUPERHERO OF SUBURBIA!

There was a drawing of a muscular superhero wearing a costume made out of black plastic trash bags. He was hoisting a dented garbage can lid over his head and about to smash an evil-looking kid in a sideways cap. The kid was brandishing a rolled-up newspaper with a sizzling fuse. The cartoon balloon coming out of Garbageman's mouth read: "I've got some bad news for you, Newspaperboy. You're about to be recycled."

"You guys?" said Sierra, sounding annoyed. "This isn't fiction. This is just a comic book."

"One that we created," said Miguel. "There's Andrew's garbageman and Kyle's newspaperboy."

"Well," said Akimi, "if the story master picked comic books for us, maybe he thinks someone on our team needs to lighten up a little." She gave a not-too-subtle nod at Sierra.

"If we want to break out first, we need the combination to this red lock," said Kyle. "So we need to step inside the comic book."

"Fine," sighed Sierra. "Let's go meet Garbageman and Newspaperboy."

They pushed open the heavy comic-book-cover door

and entered a room where the walls were flooded with screen-dot graphics of a cheerful and tidy subdivision filled with tidy homes, tidy lawns, and even tidier gardens.

Up on TV monitors mounted on each of the room's four walls, the players could see that a computer program had turned their MoCap suits into retro, 1950s-looking street clothes.

"We're in a vintage comic book," said Andrew. "A collectible. We're probably worth a ton of money right now."

"Look for something with three numbers on it," said Kyle. "Maybe a house number. The red lock had a dial like the ones on our lockers."

"We need to act out the story to find the clue," Akimi reminded him. "The answer's not going to be painted on a mailbox."

Suddenly, a holographic superhero, wearing a suit of trash bags and a fluttering shag-carpet cape, plunged out of the sky and landed right in front of the five teammates. A pair of spiky sound-effect balloons reading "VOOMP!" swirled around his work boots.

"Greetings, fellow suburbanites!" said the holographic (and extremely realistic) Garbageman, standing with both fists propped on his hips.

Heroic music swelled out of hidden speakers.

And Garbageman smelled like, well, spoiled milk mixed with dirty diapers and a rotten tuna salad sandwich.

"Smell-a-vision," said Miguel. "Mr. Lemoncello loves that stuff."

"Yeah," said Kyle, checking out the scene in the room, which had incredibly high ceilings. "The special effects are amazing."

"And immersive," said Akimi. "I feel like all of this is really real."

"That's just stupid scenery projected on the walls from high-definition video projectors," said Andrew. "Our costumes are stupid computer-generated graphics."

"So?" said Akimi. "It's still stupidly amazing."

Garbageman swatted away a few of the flies buzzing around his head and strode forward. The plastic trash bags he wore as tights rustled and crinkled. His mask was basically a dirty black sock with a pair of eyeholes cut into it. "Tell me, SIERRA RUSSELL, what is your superpower?"

Sierra shrugged. "Reading, I guess."

"Sorry. Choose another, please." The comic-book hero pointed to a hologram of a digital spinner that materialized right in front of Sierra.

"This is so random. . . ."

"Spin the wheel," said Garbageman. "And hurry. You only have ONE HOUR AND FIFTY-ONE minutes to open your FIVE remaining locks!"

24

Glancing around the room, Kyle once again looked for some kind of clue that would help them open the red lock on their codex.

Maybe a street address. A highway sign. Even a 7-Eleven. Something with numbers he could use to piece together a combination.

"Newspaperboy is headed this way," said Garbageman. "I fear he might be about to deliver some bad news!"

"Spin it, Sierra," urged Kyle, jiggling the locks on the team's codex. "Maybe your superpower will be lockpicking!"

"Fine."

Sierra reluctantly touched the holographic superpowers spinner. It immediately started to twirl, flicking a clicking pointer. Slowing down, it came to a stop on "Flight."

The perspective of the projections immediately shifted.

Kyle felt as if he and his whole team had zoomed up into the treetops.

"We're flying!" shouted Akimi. "Cool! Just like Peter Pan or the kids in Maximum Ride!"

"I want this ride to end!" moaned Sierra. "I'm afraid of heights."

"We're not really flying!" said Andrew. "It's just a trick of perspectives. Look at your feet. They're still on the ground."

"No, they're not!" screamed Sierra. "There's nothing down there but sky!"

"Because the floor turned blue. It's just an optical illusion!"

Miguel started sniffing. "Anybody else smell rotten bananas?"

"Yeah," said Kyle. "That tree over there is filled with them."

"Um, what's a banana tree doing in the middle of suburbia?" said Akimi.

"Look!" shouted Sierra. "Here comes Newspaperboy!"

The evil-looking kid in his floppy *Newsies* cap from the comic-book-cover door came trundling up the street on a rocket-powered tricycle. He was wearing a bandit mask and a striped T-shirt. He also clutched a rolled-up newspaper with a sizzling fuse in his hand.

Garbageman bounded over to block Newspaperboy's path.

"Cease and desist, Newspaperboy!" said Garbageman.

"Get outta my way, you worthless sack of trash!" The kid's voice sounded like he gargled with gravel. "I need to deliver some bad news to Granny."

"Not on my watch," said Garbageman.

"Ah, you're too old and soggy to catch me!"

Newspaperboy scooted sideways on his trike. Garbageman lunged after him, missed, and landed in a thorny rosebush that snagged his trash-bag tights.

"Need a little help," he grunted.

"Look, you guys!" said Miguel. He pointed at a tiny figure far off in the distance. Squinting, Kyle and his friends could make out an old dog in a granny dress and bonnet. She was standing on her hind legs and pushing a wobbly, creaky walker.

"*La-di-da, di-da,*" the elderly dog hummed sweetly.

"That's not what I meant when I said 'a dog with her walker,'" complained Sierra.

"Play along," said Miguel. "We need our lock combination."

"And Granny needs help!" grunted Garbageman, still trapped in the tangled rosebush. "It's up to you, SIERRA! Go rescue Granny!"

Newspaperboy zipped up the street. "Hey, Granny? I don't think you read this morning's headline. It says 'KA-BOOM!'"

"You guys?" said Kyle. "We have to help her!"

"But how?" said Andrew.

Kyle looked around. "The bananas!"

"What?" said Akimi.

"This is like that old-fashioned computer game Adventure! We have to use whatever objects we find in the story."

"Kyle's right," said Sierra, taking charge. "Grab some bananas."

"Seriously?" said Andrew.

"Yes, Andrew. They're the only weapon currently available."

The team flew to the fruit tree and started plucking holographic bananas. The fruit responded to their grabs and moved with their hands.

"The CGI effects in this room are incredible!" said Akimi.

"It doesn't matter," whined Andrew. "We'll never catch up with Newspaperboy. He's got, like, a six-block head start."

"Oh, yes, we will!" said Sierra. "Because Newspaperboy can't fly!"

Sierra gritted her teeth, leaned forward, and kicked her feet. When she did, the whole room seemed to tilt sideways, putting the team parallel to the ground in classic Superman style. Sierra swooped after the terror on the trike.

"Yee-haw!" she shouted (probably for the first time in her life).

The others yee-hawed and soared after her.

115

"This is awesome!" shouted Kyle. He could feel wind rushing past his face the way it would on a roller coaster. He leaned left and the whole room swerved sideways.

"It's like we're jets!" added Miguel.

Kyle glanced at one of the video screens. The people watching the game show on TV could see them streaking across the sky, faster than a speeding comet.

And they all had bananas gripped in their fists.

But what do bananas and rescuing a dog have to do with finding the numbers we need to open the red lock? thought Kyle.

"Attack!" shouted Sierra. "Begin banana bombardment!"

They all pelted the nasty little newsboy with fruit.

"Oh, no!" shouted Newspaperboy, looking up and shaking his fist. "It's raining bananas!"

"Throw the next volley *in front* of his tires!" cried Sierra.

"You got it!" shouted Kyle, heaving his second banana. It went *KER-SPLAT!* and split open and, since it was a hologram in a comic book, turned into a yellow sludge puddle that quickly spread out in all directions.

The tricycle skidded sideways in the slime. Newspaperboy toppled off his ride. His rolled-up tube hit the pavement and the fuse sputtered out, doused by the banana slop oozing all over the asphalt.

"You flying Lemon Heads have defeated me!" shouted Newspaperboy.

He ran away.

"Bless you, SIERRA!" said the doddering dog. "You and your league of LEMON HEADS saved me. That'll make for a much happier headline."

She hobbled away and soon disappeared.

"My job here is done," said Garbageman. "Catch you kids later!" He pointed to the sky and zoomed upward, ripping his shag-carpet cape in two and taking half the snagged rosebush with him.

"Wait a second!" said Andrew. "Where's everybody going? Somebody needs to give us a clue about how to open our red lock!"

25

"How are we supposed to open the red lock?" whined Andrew.

"The newspaper!" said Kyle. "The clue could be in it!"

"There it is," said Miguel, pointing to where it sat on the ground, soaked in banana goop.

"And it's not a hologram anymore," added Sierra. "It's real."

"They must've popped it up through the floor panels when we weren't looking," said Akimi.

"Because we need to read it to find the combination to our first lock," said Kyle.

Sierra picked up the tabloid-sized newspaper. Scanned the front page. "There's only one headline on the front: 'KA-BOOM!'"

"What about on the inside?" asked Kyle.

Sierra flipped through the pages.

"There's only three other stories on the inside pages: 'Eleven Stays the Same When Written Upside Down.' 'Twenty-One Gun Salute Goes Off by Accident.' 'Only Twenty More Days Until It's Twenty Days from Now.'"

"What a ridiculous newspaper," grumbled Andrew.

Sierra flipped the paper over and studied the back cover.

"Nothing here but a sports report." She held it up:

11-Player Football Team Wins Game 21–20

"Guess the other team missed an extra point," mumbled Miguel.

"And," said Kyle with a grin, "I think we're missing the point of this newspaper."

"Huh?" said Andrew.

"Eleven, twenty-one, twenty!" shouted Miguel. "The three numbers that were repeated in the headlines."

"Exactly," said Kyle.

"Woo-hoo!" shouted Akimi.

"Hurry!" said Andrew. "We don't have all day!"

"More like one hour and forty-eight minutes," said Akimi. She pointed to the digital countdown clock in the corner of the nearest video screen.

Kyle spun the wheel a couple of times to clear the lock, just like he'd do on his locker. "Right to eleven," he said, working the dial from zero to eleven. "Left to twenty-one."

His hands were sweaty. His fingers slippery on the knob. He wondered how the other teams were doing.

"Hurry!" This time it was Sierra saying it.

Kyle dried his fingertips on his leggings. Gave the dial its final twist.

"Right to twenty."

The lock flashed red and clicked open.

Holographic confetti and streamers fluttered down from the ceiling.

"Oh, yeah!" boomed an electronically altered video game voice accompanied by whistles, bells, and *WHOOP-WHOOP*s. "First lock? Open. Four more? Breakout!"

26

"Scan the walls for windows, doors, and mirrors," said Kyle as the Lemon Heads exited the Comic Book Room and found themselves inside a twisty, walled-off passageway.

Kyle was feeling great. He gave a quick thumbs-up to the nearest camera and mouthed, "Hiya, Mom!"

"We're like mice searching for cheese," cracked Akimi, feeling her way through the tight maze.

"What we need to look for are four more lock combinations," said Andrew. "Blue, yellow, purple, and green."

"Actually," said Miguel, who was now carrying the codex, "this yellow one needs a key."

They turned a corner and came to a junction where two black walls met. A video monitor was mounted in the angle. A grid of images filled the screen.

"Look," said Sierra. "There's Charles and his team in the Horror Room."

"Yo," said Miguel, pointing at the strip of information at the bottom of the screen, "that's only their first genre. We're winning!"

"No, we're not," said Kyle, pointing at another image on the video screen mosaic (which also contained a frame of Kyle and his teammates pointing at the screen). "The Kidzapalooza All-Stars are. See? They're in their *second* room."

On that video square, macho Peyton appeared to be wrestling a young Abraham Lincoln while comic Kai snuck up behind the lanky Illinois lawyer with a bucket labeled "Pig Slop." Haley, Gabrielle, and Jaylen were on the sidelines, cheering them on.

"Now, that really is historical fiction," said Akimi with an eye roll.

"This game is rigged!" blurted Andrew.

"Huh?" said Akimi.

"It's a Kidzapalooza game show! The Kidzapalooza All-Stars are in the lead because Mr. Lemoncello wants the Kidzapalooza kids to win!"

"No," said a voice from the ceiling. "I don't."

It was Mr. Lemoncello.

"I want an action-packed, thrill-a-minute nail-biter of a game. Might I suggest you five stop staring at all those screens and hurry along to your next genre? I myself have some more expert color commentating to do. This time, I'll comment on the differences between Apricot, Asparagus, and Forest Green in a jumbo sixty-four-color box of crayons. Toodles!"

"Mr. Lemoncello's right," said Kyle. "We need to hurry."

"Okay," said Akimi. "But to where? There's nothing here but two blank walls."

"Phones up, everybody," said Kyle.

The teammates whipped out their smartphones and activated their augmented-reality viewers.

"Red door on the left wall," reported Akimi.

"We already did red," said Kyle.

"Green window on the right!" said Miguel.

"Yes!" said Sierra, still stoked from her stint as a superhero.

"That's where we need to be," said Kyle. "We've got a green lock to open!"

He and Akimi worked together to raise the window. When everybody was safely inside the new, darkened room, they heard the window slide down behind them.

"Welcome to your second genre," said the voice in the ceiling. "There is one hour and forty-three minutes remaining in the game."

A whistle blew. Drummers beat out a cadence for a marching band. The air smelled like grass, freshly turned dirt, and then a locker room filled with BO.

"Uh-oh," muttered Miguel.

"What?"

"I think I know where we are."

"Welcome, LEMON HEADS," said the voice in the ceiling (which was suddenly a gruff man), "to sports!"

Miguel's shoulders sank. "I hate sports."

"This window," said the ceiling voice, "will give you a peek into a world you may know little about."

"I know enough to know I hate it," said Miguel.

"But," said Kyle, "we need it."

"Definitely!" added Andrew, pointing at the codex, where the green lock had, all of a sudden, started pulsing like a traffic light.

"We're looking for five letters to open this one," Kyle reminded everybody.

"Fine," said Miguel. "Let's go play some sports. I just hope it isn't dodgeball."

27

Earsplitting shrieks filled the Horror Room.

"Get away from me, Frankenstein!" shouted Morgan.

"Technically," shouted Hannah, "that's not Frankenstein. That's Frankenstein's monster. . . ."

For the first time, Charles Chiltington wondered if he'd made a huge mistake recruiting bookish geniuses instead of gamers.

His teammates were panicking.

Frankenstein's monster lurched after Morgan, chasing her around the room, which resembled the foggy nighttime streets of London. She blocked his lunges with the team's codex.

Mirabai and Hannah were stuck in what looked like a pit, dodging a swinging pendulum.

"None of this is real!" shouted Mirabai.

"Pretend!" said Charles. "Make-believe! That's what fiction is all about. It's fake!"

"Actually," said Hannah, "the finest literary fiction is humankind's attempt to understand and express its innermost—"

"Never mind!" screamed Charles. "We have to defeat Frankenstein's monster or we're never learning the combination to our first lock!"

Charles's teammate Ryan Capruso was at the control box, trying desperately to slide his "Get Out of Here Free Emergency Rescue" card into the slot. He couldn't do it because his hands were trembling. A remote-controlled bat drone had just landed on his head and claw-clamped his curly hair.

"I hate this game!" Ryan shouted. "I like reading about orcs, trolls, and Gollum. But I never wanted to meet a monster in a dark room! Get me out of here! Now!"

Finally, he jammed his GOOHFER card into the machine. A trapdoor sprang open beneath his feet. He fell through and landed with a soft thud.

"I'm good!" he shouted as the trapdoor closed. "And I'm keeping the gift cards, Charles! Later, hobbits."

"Quitters never win!" Charles fumed.

He snuck into a dark corner and, out of camera range, fired off a quick text to his father. He wasn't supposed to use his game phone for text messages. He didn't want Mr. Lemoncello disqualifying him again.

> Ignore this disaster.
> We will win in the end!

His father did not respond.

He probably wasn't even watching the show on TV.

"We need a torch!" shouted Morgan, swinging the team's codex at the monster. "Frankenstein's monster is afraid of fire."

"Is there a torch over there?" Charles called to Mirabai and Hannah.

"No. There's nothing!" said Hannah. "Except for this giant swinging-pendulum-style pizza slicer straight out of an Edgar Allan Poe story!"

"Wait," said Mirabai. "A prop just appeared in our pit. It rose up out of the floor."

"What is it?" asked Charles.

"Something that makes absolutely no sense."

"This is a Lemoncello game!" said Charles. "Get used to things not making sense."

"Okay. It looks like an antique boom box and a stack of even older CDs."

"CDs?" shrieked Morgan. "How are compact discs going to defeat Frankenstein's monster or help us find the combination to our first lock?"

"It's disco music," said Mirabai, reading the label on one of the CDs.

"Disco?" wailed Frankenstein's monster. "Noooo! Not dis-coooo!"

Of course! thought Charles. The solution to this dilemma would be wacky and goofy because the story master, Mr. Lemoncello, was wacky and goofy.

"Pop the CD into the boom box."

Grudgingly, Hannah slid the shiny CD into the music player. When she pushed the play button, loud, thumping music filled the room. *"Burn, baby, burn—disco inferno,"* singers chanted over and over and over.

"No!" screamed Frankenstein's monster. "Noooo!"

The hulking monster ran away.

Ha! Charles had been smarter than all the smarty-pants on his team. Maybe he didn't need them to win this thing. Maybe he could do it all by himself, like he'd almost done in the very first escape game. A solo victory would make his father even prouder.

"Hand me that codex," he said to Morgan.

She passed it over to him.

Charles started fidgeting with the illuminated pink lock, which had five wheels of letters.

"What are you doing?" asked Mirabai. "We haven't received a clue as to how to open it yet."

Charles shook his head. *Amateurs.* His teammates were practically worthless.

He didn't answer Mirabai.

He simply rotated the letters until they spelled out a five-letter word: "D-I-S-C-O."

The pink lock flickered, flashed, and popped open.

Holographic confetti and streamers rained down from the ceiling.

"Oh, yeah!" boomed an electronically altered video game voice accompanied by triumphant synthesized trumpets, bells, and whistles. "First lock? Open! Four more? Breakout!"

28

"Yowzers!" said Mr. Lemoncello, doing play-by-play reporting from the broadcast booth. "Here comes Mr. Touchdown! Miguel is a fantabulous footballer!"

Dr. Zinchenko was in the booth with Mr. Lemoncello, squinting in disbelief at the monitor, where a buff and speedy Miguel Fernandez, decked out in a vintage 1920s football uniform, bobbed and weaved his way through a crowd of would-be tacklers.

The computer had transformed his teammates—Kyle, Akimi, Andrew, and Sierra—into a flying wedge of three-hundred-pound blockers.

"That doesn't look like Miguel Fernandez," remarked Dr. Zinchenko. "The other children don't look like themselves, either."

"Exactamundo, Dr. Z!" exclaimed Mr. Lemoncello. "Another marvel from the world of fiction. We can see ourselves as the characters in books. In this case, I believe Miguel has become the fictional Spike Tidwell, All-American. Look at Miguel go! He's inside out and back again!"

The only part of the footballer zigzagging up the field that actually looked like Miguel was his smiling face, which was superimposed on the bulging torso and muscular legs of a fantastic fictional footballer.

"This is awesome!" Miguel shouted.

"And how are Charles Chiltington and the Bookworms doing?" asked Dr. Zinchenko.

"Well," said Mr. Lemoncello, "we're twenty minutes into the game and they've just now completed their first room."

The TV showed a slow-motion replay of Charles proudly opening his pink lock.

"Charles and his three remaining teammates are now pausing in the hallway to see how the other teams are doing. Uh-oh. Looks like Mirabai Keshap is calling it quits. She's inserting her GOOHFER card into the control box."

"Making her the second player to abandon the Bookworms team," added Dr. Zinchenko.

The camera zoomed in on Mirabai's face.

"I'm a reader, not a gamer!" she cried. "And Charles Chiltington is a jerk!"

Her eyes bugged out as the floor beneath her feet sprang open. She dropped out of sight.

"Ouch," said Mr. Lemoncello. "Bad performance

review for Charles's leadership skills. It's time to check in with Haley Daley and the rest of our Kidzapalooza All-Stars. They're deep inside their second genre, historical fiction! Having successfully wrestled Abraham Lincoln, they've moved on to the Revolutionary War!"

"Aren't they going backward in time?" said Dr. Zinchenko.

"And that's why we love fiction!" cried Mr. Lemoncello. "Where even the impossible is possible!"

The live video feed switched to Peyton McCallister talking to Alexander Hamilton.

"Alexander Hamilton," said Hamilton. "My name is Alexander Hamilton."

"I'm Peyton McCallister," said Peyton. "And nobody's done a musical about me, but just you wait. Just you wait."

"In this final chapter of their historical fiction saga," explained Dr. Zinchenko, "the Kidzapalooza All-Stars have become the youngest members of Hamilton's ragtag army of revolutionaries."

"The year is 1781," said Mr. Lemoncello. "The place? Yorktown, Virginia. The fate of the rebellion is in the All-Stars' hands. You know, Dr. Z, as any turtle in paradise will tell you, there's nothing like historical fiction to make the past seem real."

"You can say that again," said Dr. Z.

And so Mr. Lemoncello did.

On-screen, Haley Daley picked something up off the ground—one of the three real objects in the room.

"Looks like Haley's going with the pom-poms instead of the musket or the letter to Lafayette. It's a gamble, but it might work."

"Pom-poms, letter, musket," said Dr. Zinchenko. "Those were her three choices. Let's see where her choice sends this story!"

Shaking her rustling pom-poms, Haley led Jaylen and Kai in a rousing cheer.

"Huzzah! Huzzay! The Brits are up against the Chesapeake Bay! Huzzah! Huzzay! It's time to start the USA!"

"Wow!" said Mr. Lemoncello. "Here comes the white flag. The British troops are surrendering. The war is over! Haley Daley's days as a cheerleader here in Alexandriaville, not to mention her cunning intelligence, have really helped turn the tide in Yorktown."

"Indeed," added Dr. Zinchenko. "She knew exactly what to do and when to do it."

Mr. Lemoncello nodded. "Seventeen eighty-one. This victory means Lafayette will now give our All-Stars a riddle. If they can solve it, they'll unlock the *second* lock on their codex, placing them firmly in the lead. Let's listen in."

"*En haut, en bas, à droite, à droite,*" said Lafayette.

"Say what, dude?" said Peyton. He looked more confused than usual.

"Can you repeat the clue, please?" said Haley. "In English?"

"No," said Lafayette. "Zat is against zee rules. But I can repeat it in pictures!"

133

He gestured toward the wall, and a rebus puzzle appeared, floating over the battlefield:

"I'm, like, totally stumped," said Gabrielle.

"Is it something about a pig riding an elevator?" asked Kai.

"You forgot the TVs, man," said Jaylen. "It means when pigs fly, they like to watch TV on the airplane."

"Can we, like, phone a friend?" asked Gabrielle.

"Hey, hey, you guys," said Haley. "Don't worry. I speak Rebus. Kai, on the sliding lock, the combination is up, down, right, right."

Kai worked the combination.

It snapped open.

"Oh, yeah!" boomed the electronic video game voice as confetti and streamers fluttered down. "Second lock? Open! Three more? Breakout!"

"Woo-hoo!" cried Jaylen. "On to the next room!"

"Haley?" said Gabrielle through a very painful-looking smile.

"Yeah?"

"Next time, ask *me* to open the lock, not Kai," she whispered. "I should get the close-up. I've been a star way longer than him. Or, for that matter, *you*."

29

"Wait!" said Charles, peering at the screen of his phone. "There's an orange door. We need orange!"

"The door's labeled 'Mystery,'" said Morgan.

"I do not enjoy mysteries," said Hannah. "They make me anxious."

Suddenly, the burly security guard Clarence pushed open a panel in the maze wall and stepped into the narrow corridor. The panel door remained slightly ajar.

Behind Clarence, Charles could see a bank of glowing computers. The grid frames for several animated holographic characters were slowly rotating on their screens. One was a schoolteacher, three were schoolkids, and one was a sleuth in a Sherlock Holmes hat holding a magnifying glass.

Characters for the Mystery Room, Charles decided.

"Excuse me, kids," said Clarence, sidling past them. "Need a quick bathroom break. Howdy, Charles."

The security guard ambled around a corner.

"Go into the mystery story," Charles told his teammates. "I'll meet you there."

"Where are you going?" asked Hannah.

"I need to go to the bathroom, too," said Charles, loud enough for any microphones to hear.

"Well, hurry!" said Hannah. "There's only ninety minutes left in the game!"

Hannah and Morgan stepped into the Mystery Room.

Charles glanced up at the ceiling.

There was one camera, but it was aimed at the door.

It was positioned right above a multipanel video screen showing Haley's team completing their second room. A meter icon indicated that Keeley's team was seventy-five percent done with *their* second genre.

Charles's team was losing.

Desperate times called for desperate measures.

Charles casually exited to the left so the camera would think he was simply following Clarence to the bathroom. But as soon as he was out of that camera's range, Charles spun around, hugged the wall, slipped underneath the camera, and inched his way back to the control room door.

Just like in a spy movie, Charles thought. *I am awesome!*

Inside the dark room were three dozen or more screens, plus all sorts of humming hard drives and blinking servers.

This must be the Narrative Drive supercomputer, he reasoned. *The brains behind the whole game.*

He saw a monitor with "Mystery Solution" streaming across the bottom of its frame. It showed a flower pen jabbed into the gravel at the bottom of a classroom turtle's terrarium.

Real props. Not holograms. Just like the real CDs and CD player back in the Horror Room.

"Welcome back from recess, class," Charles heard the teacher character say through a monitor when Hannah and Morgan stepped into the mystery story. They joined the three holographic schoolkids, all of them trying really hard not to look guilty.

The teacher was standing in front of a chalkboard with "The Case of the Purloined Pen" written on it.

"Time for me to grade your homework," she said, opening a desk drawer. "Wait. Oh, no! Someone stole my pen!"

DUN-DUN-DUN! music blasted out of concealed speakers.

"Whodunit?" asked the detective, emerging from the shadows. "With your help, HANNAH CHUNG, I think I can solve this crime."

"Um, okay," said Hannah. "But I'm not very good at mysteries. . . ."

Of course she isn't, thought Charles. None of his eighth-grade geniuses were very good at anything except reading books, and so far, this game didn't involve reading or real books.

I picked the wrong players.

I need to do all the work!

He darted out of the control room and retraced his stealthy moves so viewers would think he was coming from the bathroom.

"Interrogate these suspects, HANNAH," he heard the detective say.

"Morgan, too?" asked Hannah.

"It's your story," said the teacher. "Write it any way you choose. Just find my flower pen!"

Charles dashed into view from the left, pushed open the Mystery Room door, and stepped into the room.

"Ah! Welcome, CHARLES," said the detective. "Perhaps you can be of some—"

"The flower pen is in the turtle terrarium. Over there in the corner."

Charles raced to the terrarium and plucked out the pen.

"But how did you solve the mystery so quickly?" marveled the teacher. "You didn't interview a single witness! You didn't search for any evidence."

Charles shrugged. "I read a lot of Hardy Boys and Nancy Drew."

"But whodunit?" asked the detective.

Charles tried to think the way Mr. Lemoncello, the story master, might think. "Um, the detective. Everybody else was outside during recess."

"Phooey!" said the detective as handcuffs appeared on his wrists. "You outsmarted me, Charles!"

"Indeed. I do that quite often."

All of the holographic characters vanished.

"That's it?" said Hannah. "That's the end of our detective story?"

"Yep," said Charles. "Because we skipped all the boring clues-and-witnesses stuff in the middle."

"But where's *our* clue?" asked Morgan. "How do we open the blinking orange lock on our codex?"

Charles examined the flower pen. It looked homemade.

"Somebody just attached this flower to the top of this pen with green florist tape."

"So?" said Morgan.

"So, this is a Uniball Impact 207."

"So?" Hannah said it this time.

Charles rolled his eyes.

These book nerds are so useless.

"So, the orange lock on our codex is a three-digit lock. Roll the wheels to two, zero, and seven."

Morgan, who was carrying the boxy book, worked the combination.

A cluster of LEDs inside the orange lock started blinking. It slid open.

"Oh, yeah!" blared the video game voice. "Second lock? Open! Three more? Breakout!"

Confetti fell. Streamers unfurled. And, from the live-feed monitor, Charles could hear the audience outside cheering.

"Yes!" he said, giving himself a hearty arm pump.

That was when the phone in his pocket started to vibrate.

Charles ducked out of camera range.

He glanced at the glowing screen of his phone.

His father *was* watching the game show on TV.

He'd just sent Charles a text:

> Why are you celebrating?
> You still have three rooms to go!

30

"Onward, team!" Miguel shouted heroically, racing up the football field as the fictitious Spike Tidwell, All-American, to score yet another touchdown.

A buzzer sounded.

The game was over.

"Look, you guys," said Kyle, pointing to the green lock on their codex. Instead of throbbing, it blinked. "I think, by winning the game, we just completed our story."

Miguel stared up at the live-feed screen. "Aw, man, we all just look like us again. I loved being Spike Tidwell, All-American."

"Well, I didn't like running that fast," whined Andrew. "It couldn't've been good for my heart."

"It was just make-believe, you guys," said Akimi.

"Maybe," said Miguel. "But the whole time we were playing football, I imagined I really was Spike Tidwell!"

"That's what good books do," said Sierra. "They let you become someone else for a few hundred pages."

"But what about our clue?" said Kyle, checking out the live feed of the game on a monitor. "There's only ninety minutes left and the Kidzapalooza All-Stars have already finished their second room. We still need to open our second lock."

"What kind is it?" asked Andrew.

"Five letters. We need a five-letter word. . . ."

" 'S-P-I-K-E,' " said Miguel. "Spike!"

Kyle tried it.

It didn't work.

"I know!" said Andrew. "Touchdown!"

"Yo," said Miguel. "That's like nine letters."

"Congratulicitations!" said a flickering image of Mr. Lemoncello floating in the center of the room. "If you are seeing this prerecorded greeting, that means (a) I paid the electric bill this month, and (b) you have successfully completed your sports story without spending a year down yonder. Time now for a riddle . . ."

"I hate riddles," said Andrew.

"Shhh!" said Akimi. "This is going to be our green lock clue."

"You are in Luigi World," said Mr. Lemoncello. "There is a mirror but no reflection. There is pepper but no salt. There is a door, yet no entrance or exit. What is everybody's favorite football food? Good luck, gamers!"

Mr. Lemoncello's image disappeared and was replaced by the words from his riddle.

Sierra turned to Kyle. "What's the answer, Kyle?"

"Not sure," said Kyle. His mind was racing. He stared at the words. Tried to make sense of the nonsense. "I'm working on it."

"Well," said Akimi, "could you work a little faster? The Kidzapalooza team is moving on to their *third* room."

"Something we should be doing!" said Andrew.

Kyle blocked out the noise and focused on the words.

LUIGI WORLD

There is a mirror but no reflection.
There is pepper but no salt.
There is a door, yet no entrance or exit.
What is everybody's favorite football food?

"The things that are in Luigi World are a mirror, pepper, and a door," mumbled Kyle.

"And the things that aren't there are a reflection, salt, entrance, and exit," said Akimi. "We all got that far, Kyle, because, hello, we can read!"

Kyle nodded. "Mirror, pepper, and door. What do they have in common? What's the connection?"

"Well," said Sierra, " 'mirror,' 'pepper,' and 'door' all have double letters in them!"

"Yes!" said Akimi. "And the other words don't!"

"Brilliant!" shouted Kyle.

"So what's the answer, bro?" asked Miguel.

"What's 'everybody's favorite football food'?" said Andrew.

Kyle thought. "It has to be a word with double letters in it."

"It also has to be a food," said Akimi.

"Beets!" shouted Sierra.

"Um, nobody really eats those when they watch football," said Akimi.

"How about seeds?" said Miguel. "You know, pumpkin seeds."

"Or Peeps! Those marshmallow thingies," said Akimi.

Kyle snapped his fingers. "Pizza! 'P-I-double-Z-A'!"

He rotated the five letter wheels on the green lock to P-I-Z-Z-A. The lock slid open.

"Here comes the confetti!" said Sierra.

"Oh, yeah!" thundered the video game voice. "Second lock? Open! Three more? Breakout!"

"Woo-hoo," cheered Akimi. "Way to go, team!"

"Phones up, everybody!" shouted Kyle, eager to keep the game rolling. "We still have blue, yellow, and purple locks to go!"

31

As Kyle and his team roamed the maze between rooms, they had their phones up and their augmented-reality apps running.

"I see a purple door!" said Akimi. "No. Wait. It moved."

"How about yellow or blue?" said Kyle.

"Here's a yellow window!" said Miguel, tapping the wall. "Nope, it's gone."

"My blue mirror just disappeared, too," said Sierra.

"What's going on?" whined Andrew. "Why are we, all of a sudden, playing Whack-A-Mole?"

Kyle gestured toward a video screen mounted in a nook where two walls met.

"Commercial break," he said.

The game was no longer on the live feed. Instead, there was a promo for *Hey, Hey, Haley*, which apparently had all new episodes starting next week.

"Oh, good. They used the best clip!"

Haley and the rest of the Kidzapalooza All-Stars joined the Lemon Heads in the hallway.

"That's going to be hysterical, Hales," said Kai, the goofy comic, watching the promo. "Excellent physical shtick!"

"Thanks, Kai."

"Was that a real vat of mayonnaise you just fell into?"

"Yeah."

"I don't do slapstick or gross-out humor on my show," said Gabrielle. "It's too immature."

"Maybe that's why your ratings are slipping like they stepped on a banana peel," sniped Jaylen.

"Excuse me?"

Jaylen threw up his hands. "I'm just saying."

"You guys?" said Peyton, gesturing toward Kyle and his teammates. "Civilian alert. I know we're off-air, but you don't want your dirty underpants showing up on some Ohio kid's Twitter feed."

"My underpants aren't dirty, Peyton!" fumed Gabrielle.

"Uh, hey," said Kyle, waving at the celebs. They were clustered at one end of the hall, Kyle and his friends at the other. "Guess we're having a slight delay."

"Commercials!" said Andrew. "Don't you just hate them?"

"Not really, dude," said Jaylen. "They pay our salaries."

"So, you guys have finished two rooms?" said Kyle.

"To the max!" growled Peyton.

"How about you guys?" Haley asked Kyle.

"Two."

"Guess we're all tied up."

Suddenly, a wall panel flipped open.

Out came Charles and his two remaining teammates, Morgan Peden and Hannah Chung.

The tight corridor was extremely crowded.

"We just finished our second room!" Charles crowed. "We're tied with you losers!"

"Dude?" said Jaylen. "If we're tied, then nobody's a loser. Read a dictionary."

"Oh, I will. Right after I defeat, trounce, and thrash you, Mr. Swell, if that really is your name."

"Nah. It's more of a stage name. Has pizzazz!" Then Jaylen made another dab move.

"Love your show," said Morgan.

"I love *yours*," Hannah said to Peyton.

"Thanks," said Peyton, switching into super-suave mode. "Have we met?"

"Peyton?" said Gabrielle. "Hello? I'm standing right here."

"And now," boomed Mr. Lemoncello's voice, "back to our game!"

Music swelled. The live-feed monitor showed all thirteen contestants stuck in the same tiny corridor.

"Oh, my," said Mr. Lemoncello in a voice-over. "It's a traffic jam, which, by the way, tastes terrible on toast."

"With eighty minutes left," said Dr. Zinchenko, "it's time to light up those windows, doors, and mirrors!"

"There's a purple door!" blurted Akimi. "And it's staying still!"

"There's ours!" shouted Haley. "Catch you later, Kyle!"

"See you when you break out," said Kyle. "After us!"

"Get out of my way, both of you!" said Charles, elbowing between Kyle and Haley.

"Wait for us!" shouted Morgan and Hannah, trailing after him. Charles and his teammates scrambled to the far end of the hall and climbed through a glistening golden window.

Haley and her crew found the door they were looking for and disappeared.

"Our purple door is down there!" said Akimi, leading the way.

"Another door," said Andrew. "Looks like we need to enter another weird world."

"You ever notice that books actually look like doors?" said Miguel. "You open up the cover just like you'd open a door."

"Come on, you guys," said Kyle. "We've caught up with the Kidzapalooza team. We have a real shot at winning this thing."

Kyle tucked the locked book box under his arm and led the way into his team's third Fictionasium room.

"So, what's our genre this time?" wondered Sierra as the team made their way down an ultraviolet corridor that made their teeth glow.

That was when the purple door magically slid shut and twinkly *GLING-GLING* music jingled out of the ceiling speakers.

"Uh-oh," muttered Akimi. "This better not be what I think it is."

Lights dimmed. Projections turned the walls into a magical land of gently rolling hills made of green gumdrops dusted with sparkling sugar. Multiple rainbows filled the sky, where all the puffy clouds resembled happy, fluffy bunnies. Bluebirds chirped merrily in the branches of the trees. From off on the horizon, a hologram of a pink unicorn with a glistening, wispy mane and sparkly spiral horn pranced to the center of the room. A narwhal rose up from the floor.

"Gag me now," sighed Akimi.

"Welcome, dear readers," said the airy-fairy unicorn, dipping into a four-legged curtsy, "to fairy tales!"

"And," added the narwhal, sounding like it had a head cold, "a special welcome to you, Princess AKIMI."

32

Up on the video monitor on the other side of the golden window, Charles saw what he hoped his father saw: a graphic showing that his team was tied for the lead!

Yes! thought Charles. *I am a true Chiltington. I will not lose, no matter the cost!*

"Welcome to historical fiction, BOOKWORMS," said the soothing voice in the ceiling.

Charles looked up at the speakers. "Good afternoon, ma'am. Could you kindly jump to the part of your computerized conversation where you tell us how to open this golden lock?"

There was a beat of silence.

And then the voice in the ceiling said, "Welcome to historical fiction, BOOKWORMS."

"We can't skip to the ending, Charles," said Hannah.

"Why not? It's what I do whenever I read a book."

Morgan shook her head. "Seventh graders," she muttered.

"The Kidzapalooza All-Stars already opened their historical fiction lock, so it can't be that hard," said Charles, studying the game action on the room's flat-screen TVs. "Now they're inside science fiction."

Charles and his teammates watched as Haley Daley used a ray gun (like something out of an arcade game) to blast a squad of evil aliens that kept popping up on a moonscape. The alien commander was holding the keys to a rocket ship Haley and her team needed for their intergalactic adventure.

Haley blasted him in the belly. He made deflating Pac-Man noises and dropped the rocket ship keys.

"She's good," said Hannah.

"And look," said Morgan. "There go the Lemon Heads. They're all riding unicorns and narwhals. Except for Miguel Fernandez. He's flying on a baby dragon."

"So cool," said Morgan wistfully. "I sort of wish I were on their team. . . ."

"Yeah," said Hannah. "Me too."

"Come on, you two," barked Charles. "We've caught up with the leaders. There's no time to waste!"

Charles wished he'd gotten a peek at this room when he was in the control room. Knowing the answers before you took a test always helped move things along.

He took one step forward.

And froze.

Because cannons started booming in the distance. Somewhere, a marching band was playing "The Battle Hymn of the Republic." Charles could smell gunpowder wafting on the humid breeze. Images appeared on the walls, turning the room into the smoldering countryside of Gettysburg, Pennsylvania. The date "July 3, 1863" floated over the scenery, then disappeared.

"I have a bad feeling about this," moaned Hannah.

A somber holographic figure in a long frock coat and stovepipe hat strode to the center of the room.

"It's Abraham Lincoln!" gasped Morgan.

"Welcome, book-loving friends," said the holographic Lincoln. "You know, my best friend is a person who will give me a book I have not read. For all I have learned, I learned from books."

"Sir?" said Charles. "No disrespect, but we're kind of in a hurry. Can we skip the folksy platitudes and cut to the chase? What do we need to do in this room?"

The Lincoln hologram blinked and shuddered as if it were fast-forwarding through its programmed preamble.

"Thank you, BOOKWORMS, for volunteering to serve in the Union Army!" said Lincoln, having skipped ahead in his script. "To turn the tide here at Gettysburg, you must find nine items hidden in the woods. A tin coffee cup. My spare stovepipe hat. A belt. A saber. A boot. A rifle. A glove. A tent. And, of course, an envelope with my Gettysburg Address, which I seem to have misplaced, I must humbly confess, at an unknown address."

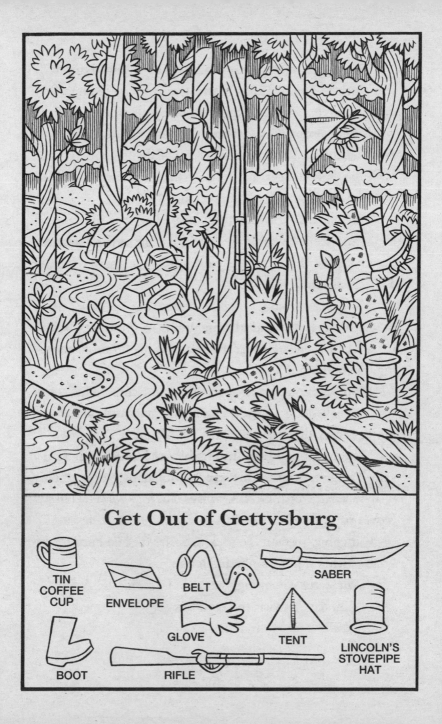

Get Out of Gettysburg

TIN COFFEE CUP

ENVELOPE

BELT

SABER

GLOVE

TENT

LINCOLN'S STOVEPIPE HAT

BOOT

RIFLE

Charles shook his head and heaved a sigh. Nine hidden objects? That was too many items for any team to find quickly. Even a group of gamers like Kyle Keeley and his crew, who probably did those hidden picture puzzles in *Highlights* every time they went to the dentist.

Charles's meager team of two book nerds needed another hint.

That meant *he* needed to sneak back to the control room and see if he could find the solution to the historical fiction puzzle the same way he'd found the answer for the Mystery Room.

"Godspeed," said Lincoln, fading out of view. "And please be sure you find all nine items in the forest before General Lee sends George Pickett and his infantry charging up yonder hill."

More cannons bombarded the landscape. The room was so realistic, it sprayed clumps of mud and dirt at the players every time the fake ground exploded.

"We're going to be in the middle of Pickett's Charge?" said Morgan, wiping dirt specks out of her eyes. "This is why I hate history. It's noisy. There's horses. Things blow up."

Clutching his team's codex, Charles dashed back to the window they'd just climbed through.

"Where are you going?" asked Hannah.

"I, uh, have to visit the facilities."

"Again?" said Hannah.

"I drank too much soda pop prior to the game's commencement. Carry on. Try to find those nine items. I'll be back in a flash."

And, he thought, *if all goes as planned, I will bring back the solution to Abraham Lincoln's ridiculous puzzle.*

33

"Yippee!" cried Sierra. "We're flying again!"

"Isn't it awesome?" said Kyle.

He and his teammates were soaring through make-believe cotton candy clouds on two flying unicorns, two airborne narwhals, and one baby dragon.

"This is ridiculous!" whined Andrew. "Narwhals can't fly!"

"Except in this story!" shouted Kyle. "Giddyup, nar-whal!"

"Wheeee!" said Sierra, gliding along on her glittering unicorn. Every time it passed gas, the unicorn created a new rainbow.

"Narwhals are sea creatures!" Andrew insisted, holding on to his ride's opalescent spiral tusk. "Like whales. Whales can't fly."

"Just go with the flow, bro," said Miguel from his saddle on the back of the baby dragon.

The puffy cloud projections on the walls slowed down. The rainbows faded from view.

"We're coming in for a landing," said Kyle. He could see a multiturreted castle cresting a green hilltop far off in the distance. It reminded him of the one at Disney World. He knew he should be thinking about the purple lock with its directional knob, but he had to admit, he was totally getting into this story.

The holographic mythical creatures floated down, depositing the five members of the Lemon Heads team in a medieval village straight out of a fairy tale.

All the quaint cottages had flower boxes outside their leaded windows. Their roofs were thatched with straw. There was a church with a steeple, as well as a bustling square filled with stalls where vendors hawked all sorts of medieval merchandise. Kyle immediately started scanning the scenery, looking for clues.

"Good luck, Princess AKIMI," neighed the unicorns.

All the magical beasts fluttered up and flew away.

"Did yon unicorn call ye a princess?" asked a scruffy peasant woman toting a pitchfork.

"Aye," said the butcher, baker, and candlestick maker. "We heard it, too!"

"I don't want to be a princess," said Akimi. "I don't

157

like gowns. Or jewels. Or going to balls. Or being rescued by some guy with shiny teeth."

"Well," said Kyle, "maybe you can be a new kind of princess."

"The kind that uses her girl power and sets all the peasants free!" said Sierra.

"Okay," said Akimi. "That might work."

"But," said Andrew, pointing at a screen that showed the players what the TV audience was seeing, "right now, it seems *we're* peasants. Look at us. Dressed in tattered rags."

"Smelling like horse manure," said Kyle, waving his hand under his nose.

Miguel nodded. "Smell-a-vision. A little goes a long way."

"Uh-oh," said Akimi.

A hologram of a handsome young prince with shiny teeth approached on a prancing white steed.

"Welcome to my nightmare. . . ."

"What ho!" the prince cried out, his dazzling blue eyes locked on Akimi. "Who be this lovely lass?"

"She be Akimi," said Andrew.

"But why, fair princess, are you dressed like a milk-maid?"

Akimi looked at her clothes on the video monitor. "Is that what I am? I thought I was the Swiss Miss lady from the front of the hot cocoa box."

The prince glided down gracefully from his gilded saddle and doffed his crown at Akimi. "Thou art no milkmaid. Thou art a thief! For, verily, thy beauty hath stolen my heart."

Akimi turned to Kyle and gave him another "gag me" gesture. "This is why I hate fairy tales. They're way too mushy."

"It's your story," Kyle whispered back. "Take it where you want to go."

"How about the toilet? So I can hurl?"

"Can we *please* figure out how to open the purple lock first?" whined Andrew.

"Okay, okay," said Akimi. She tried to act like the princesses she'd seen in Disney movies. "What is it you desire, fair prince?"

"Why, your hand in marriage, milady."

"Plot twist!" shouted Miguel.

Suddenly, four young men carrying a sedan chair on poles raced into the village square. They were animatronic mannequins. So was the royal person they carried on a portable throne: a sour-looking, shrunken old man with a scraggly gray beard and a tilted crown. His crown, made up of dozens of tiny mirrors, was blindingly bright.

"Son Dirk," the robotic king cried to the holographic prince, "what goes on here?"

"Why, Father, be merry, for I am to marry!"

"Pah! As your king and father, I forbid thee to wed this penniless peasant!"

Kyle nudged Akimi. "Act. Play the part. Three more locks and *boom!* We break out of the library!"

159

Akimi rolled her eyes. Took a deep breath.

"Sire, I wish to wed your son. But only in a totally make-believe, not-real sort of way."

"Please, Father!" beseeched Prince Dirk. "Give us your blessing."

"No!" cried the king. "I object!"

"But it is all I ever wished for upon a star," pleaded his son.

"Seriously?" said Akimi. "We only met like two minutes ago. . . ."

"Stay in character, Akimi," coached Sierra. "Just think, 'purple lock, purple lock.' "

"All right already." Akimi turned to the king. "What must I do to win your son's hand?"

"Your kind and gentle words have softened my hard heart," said the king. "I shall give thee one chance." He pulled two slips of parchment and a feathered pen out of a velvet pouch. "On one of these, I shall write 'Marriage.' On the other, 'Death.' Whichever slip of paper thou shalt take from my hand shall seal thy fate!"

"Thank you, Father," said the prince. "That seems fair."

"Dirk?" said Akimi. "You're pretty horrible at this handsome-prince stuff."

"Thank you, Princess AKIMI," he said cheerfully.

The king started to scribble.

The prince batted his eyes in eager anticipation.

"Psst," said Kyle.

"What?" said Akimi.

"Check out the reflections in the king's crown."

Akimi glanced at the miniature mirrors ringing the mannequin monarch's head and saw what Kyle had seen: The king had written the same word on both slips of paper.

No matter which one Akimi chose, her fate would be the same.

Death!

34

Looking for a hint that would help his team solve the puzzle of the Civil War story, Charles quickly retraced his steps through the Mystery Room, which was now nothing but an empty black-box theater with bare, blank walls.

This whole thing is nothing but a giant, ridiculous video game, he thought.

And yet it was a giant, ridiculous video game Charles planned to win—in less than seventy minutes!

He came out of the Mystery Room and glanced at the video screen, with its mosaic of images charting the game's progress.

The Kidzapalooza All-Star crew was on the deck of a rocking and pitching spaceship, trying to outblast the alien spacecraft bombarding them with laser beams.

Off in Fairy Tale Land, Akimi Hughes was chatting with a guy who looked like a king.

Meanwhile, *his* two remaining teammates were thrashing around in the fake forest of Gettysburg, dodging cannonball blasts and mud clods while not finding a single one of the nine hidden objects, even though Charles could clearly see Abraham Lincoln's spare stovepipe hat.

For the sake of the overhead camera, Charles pretended to dash left, once again, to the bathroom.

Then he clung to the wall and sidestepped his way back toward the master control room.

"Yes, Dr. Z," he heard the security guard say behind the wall. "I saw that, too. Maybe Charles had to go to the bathroom again."

"Clarence?" said a familiar voice through a tinny walkie-talkie-type speaker.

"Yes, Mr. Lemoncello?"

"We're in another commercial break, so I can chat without everyone in TV Land hearing our conversation. I suspect poor Charles has had enough. Half of his teammates have quit. He may have used his GOOHFER card. But he hasn't tumbled out of the building."

"You think maybe he dropped down but the undulating floor didn't undulate?" asked Clarence. "You think he's stuck down there?"

"It's a distinct possibility," said Mr. Lemoncello.

"I'll go check it out."

"Thank you, Clarence."

Charles heard keys jangling.

He scooched as far as he could into the shadows.

Clarence pushed open the wall, came into the hallway, knelt down, raised the corner on a square of carpet, and, after finding the right key on the cluttered ring clipped to his belt, opened up a door in the floor. He squeezed through the narrow opening and climbed down a steep set of stairs. As his head disappeared, he reached up and pulled the floor panel shut behind him.

Charles quickly tiptoed into the Narrative Drive super-computer control room.

There were no cameras. Nobody could see what he was doing!

He checked out the game displays.

His team was still running around the battlefield of Gettysburg.

"Charles?" he heard Morgan say. "Where are you? You're supposed to be our captain."

Another cannon blast boomed.

Charles searched the computer-generated backdrop for the Gettysburg scene and tried to find the nine hidden objects.

Charles noted where everything was hidden, then checked out the progress meters under the sci-fi and fantasy monitors. Both stories were "85% complete."

The meter under "Historical Fiction" had barely climbed out of the red. That story was only "5% complete."

We're going to lose!

His phone started buzzing again.

It was another text message from his father.

> Find a way to sabotage the others.
> FAST!

Charles felt a warm happiness flood through his whole body.

He's coaching me.

Charles's father had never coached him before. Not in baseball, football, or soccer. Not on his homework or extracurricular activities. Not even on weekends.

But now, glued to the TV, his father suddenly seemed interested in what Charles was doing.

He was offering his advice.

"Don't worry, Father," Charles said to the empty room. "We're gonna win this thing!"

35

"You guys?" Akimi whispered. "Can that kooky old king really kill me?"

"Probably not," said Kyle. "But even if he can, in most video games you get three lives."

"But don't you have to disintegrate in between?"

"Usually. And then there's the *BLOOP-BLOOP-BLOOP* video death music. . . ."

"Oh, joy."

"Hear ye, hear ye," wheezed the king. "Yon peasant girl must pick one piece of parchment. Marriage or death? Death or marriage? The choice is thine!"

"Um, team meeting?" said Akimi.

"Granted!" said the king. "But be quick about it."

Akimi huddled with Kyle, Miguel, Sierra, and Andrew.

"Need a little help," said Akimi. "He wrote 'Death' on

both papers. So no matter which one I pick, I'm basically toast."

"Well," said Andrew. "I don't think they can actually kill you. After all, this is just a story."

"But," said Miguel, "if they declare her 'dead,' I don't think we're going to get the clue we need to open the purple lock."

"Plus," said Akimi, "I'd probably have to disintegrate."

"That would slow us down," said Andrew.

"It's definitely a conflict," said Sierra.

"There has to be a solution," said Kyle. "This is just another riddle."

He worked the puzzle in his head. It reminded him of the final riddle in the Library Olympics game. He had to think outside the box.

Suddenly, it hit him!

Of course!

He whispered in Akimi's ear.

"Genius!" she said. "Thanks, Kyle."

"Hey, what are friends for?"

"Making sure I never get stuck in a sappy fairy tale like this again!"

Akimi strode forward.

"Very well, Good King Whatsyourface. I shall now pluck a parchment from thy paw."

She yanked a slip of paper out of the grinning king's hand.

"What doth it portend, Princess AKIMI?" wondered the lovestruck prince. There were cartoonish cuddling doves and Valentine's Day hearts floating around his head. "Are we to be wed or are thee to be dead?"

"You tell me, pal." She balled up the paper into a wad, stuffed it into her mouth, chewed a little, and swallowed.

The prince's shoulders sank. "Now we shall ne'er knoweth our destiny."

"Sure you will," said Kyle. "There were *two* slips of paper, remember? One said 'Death'; the other said 'Marriage.' So, Mr. King, which do you have in your hand— 'Death' or 'Marriage'?"

The dummy king's eye twitched.

So did his waxy left nostril.

Akimi and Kyle had him trapped. He'd have to show his slip of paper and say "Death," or all the villagers would know the game was rigged.

"Why, it says 'Death,'" the king finally announced, trying his best to sound dignified instead of annoyed.

"Huzzah!" shouted the prince. "We are to be wed, Princess AKIMI."

The bell in the church steeple struck one.

The bell ringer stuck his head out of the belfry.

"Hear ye, hear ye!" he cried. "The clock hath struck one. The game is halfway done!"

"Oh, yeah!" echoed the video game voice. "Halftime!"

"Yo," said Miguel. "We only have one hour left to finish this room and the next two!"

The prince wiggled his eyebrows at Akimi. "We also needeth to plan our nuptials!"

A jester, dressed all in purple, with bells jingling off the tips of his hat, leapt into the square. "First, good sir and lady, thou must learn the wedding dance!"

"Kyle?" said Akimi. "I don't want to do a wedding dance. I just want the lock combination!"

Kyle grinned. "That's why we should stick around and learn the dance."

"Why?" demanded Akimi.

"Because," said Kyle, tapping the glowing purple lock on the codex, "your dance instructor just happens to be wearing *purple*!"

36

Okay, Charles told himself. *You're in the control room. That means you can control everything—the game, the Fictionasium, maybe even the whole library!*

He checked out the array of buttons on the main panel. One was labeled "Lockdown."

He pressed it.

KATHUNKs, KERTHUDs, and *CLINKs* rumbled through the halls.

"All entrances to the Fictionasium, including those in the floor, are now sealed," said a soothing voice in the ceiling. "No one may enter. Exits are still permitted."

Nobody could come in.

No security guards, no nosy librarians, no Mr. Lemoncello.

Charles could do whatever he wanted. But he had to hurry. There was only one hour left in the game. He had to open three more locks and break out of the library before anybody else.

He looked at his team in the Historical Fiction Room on a monitor labeled "Active Story Window." They hadn't gotten any further.

The cheat sheet for Gettysburg wouldn't be enough to guarantee victory.

Maybe his father was correct.

Maybe he needed a new plan.

He remembered another *Art of War* quote his father said all the time: "The greatest victory is that which requires no battle."

For Charles to win, the others needed to lose.

He could follow his father's advice and sabotage them!

He could use the Narrative Drive to add things to the other teams' stories that would scare them into dropping out of the game.

Once they were gone (probably within the next fifteen minutes), Charles would miraculously reappear in the maze, solve a few puzzles with his teammates (with answers supplied by the Narrative Drive), open his codex, break out of the library, and be declared the winner.

His eyes adjusted to the dim light inside the control room. He examined his surroundings more closely.

Below the command console, he found a bookshelf filled with thick binders. He pulled one out. The cover was labeled "Narrative Drive Quick Start Guide."

Charles flipped through the pages. It was written like

easy-to-understand board game instructions. According to the user manual, he could add characters to any "story in progress" simply by scrolling through the "story master" options on the main command-and-control terminal.

He looked at that terminal and, maneuvering a second mouse, clicked a link labeled "Monsters." Up popped an alphabetical list of available creatures: banshee, bigfoot, gargoyle, gremlin, Medusa, Minotaur. The list went on and on.

He clicked "Minotaur," a monster from Greek mythology.

The screen blinked, and up came a question and text box: "ACTION?"

Charles pulled out the keyboard tray and typed in his command: "WREAK HAVOC."

He hit return.

He heard Hannah and Morgan scream.

Because a holographic Minotaur, half man and half bull, had just charged into their forest.

"I thought this was the Battle of Gettysburg," shouted Morgan, "not Bull Run!"

The Minotaur snorted and, scratching the dirt with its hooves, aimed its horns at Charles's teammates.

Oops, thought Charles. *Didn't mean to do that . . .*

Instead of sabotaging the other teams, he'd turned on his own because, he quickly reasoned, the Historical Fiction Room was in the Active Story Window. He flipped through the manual. Yep. He was right.

Your commands will only alter the story room currently displayed in the Active Story Window. To modify a different story, you must first click and drag it onto the ASW screen.

Charles watched the final two members of his hand-picked genius squad race to the nearest game terminal and insert their GOOHFER cards. The trapdoor sprang open and slammed shut twice. Morgan and Hannah had officially dropped out of the game.

That's it, Charles thought. *I'm done. There's no way for the Bookworms to win, because there aren't any more Bookworms left in the game!*

Then it hit him.

Except me.

I'm still here. Chiltingtons never need a team. We win on our own terms!

He glanced up at the game clock.

There were fifty-eight minutes left.

He needed to hurry.

Kyle Keeley's Lemon Heads would be the next team to receive an unexpected visitor from the Fictionasium's new story master, Charles Chiltington!

37

"Okay, jester person," Akimi said to the guy in the purple tights. "Teach us the steps."

"It is simple," said the jester. "Much like ye hokey-pokey. You bounce up, you bend down, you skip left, you hop right, and then you tug with all your might."

"Up, down, left, right!" said Miguel. "That's our lock combination!"

The purple lock was a directional lock. There were no numbers or letters on the round face. Just a knob to be pushed up, down, and sideways.

Kyle worked the dial up, down, left, and right. He tugged down. *GLING-GLING* music tinkled on a harp. Glitter sprinkled from the sky. The shackle opened.

"Oh, yeah!" roared the video game voice. "Lock three? Open! Two more? Breakout!"

"Excellent!" said Akimi. "We are so out of here!"

"Come on," said Kyle. "We only have fifty-seven more minutes."

"What's left?" asked Sierra.

"Blue and yellow. Blue is a skinny, three-number combination lock—like on a suitcase. The yellow lock needs a key."

Kyle led the way toward the exit.

"Excuseth me?" cried the prince. "Wherefore art thou going?"

"We're needed in another village," said Kyle. "More riddles to solve."

"But AKIMI and I are to be wed."

"Not gonna happen," said Akimi. "This fairy tale is going to have a happy ending. For me, anyway."

Suddenly, the way forward was blocked by a holographic troop of Civil War soldiers and a flickering flock of flying monkeys.

"You no-account pie eaters heard the prince," said one of the soldiers. "Not one step farther or we'll knock you into a cocked hat."

"What are Civil War soldiers doing in the middle of a fairy tale?" said Andrew, throwing up his arms in exasperation. "What kind of cataloging system are they using back here?"

"There could be bugs in the Narrative Drive supercomputer," said Miguel. "I heard Mr. Lemoncello and Mr. Raymo talking about it the other day. There's a way to override it, but you need two keys. . . ."

"Thou canst not refuse my love, fairest AKIMI!" shouted the prince.

"Canst and didst," said Akimi. "Kyle? We need to leave this room. Like five minutes ago!"

"This way," said Kyle.

The flying monkeys screeched and squawked and flapped their mammoth wings. They hovered overhead and dropped wet wads of something mucky and stinky on Kyle and his crew.

Great, thought Kyle. *My brothers are watching this and laughing their butts off. No, the whole world is watching and laughing.*

"Are those stupid monkeys splattering us with monkey poo?" whined Andrew.

"I think it's just simulated poop," said Sierra.

"Mixed with smell-a-vision," added Miguel.

"Just remember, you guys," said Kyle, "none of this is real."

"Well," said Akimi, scooping a chunk of soggy artificial monkey gunk out of her hair, "it sure feels and smells real."

"But these guys are just holograms!" said Kyle. "We can run right through them."

"Then let's do it!" cried Akimi.

All five Lemon Heads charged forward, flailing their arms and screaming, "Aarrrrrrgh! Out of our way! Coming through!"

The team slipped through the horde of attackers as if they were nothing more than a bank of fog.

The Lemon Heads made it out of the exit and into the maze.

There were no angry princes, rifle-toting soldiers, or airborne monkeys in the corridors of the Fictionasium, mostly because Charles hadn't found the instruction manual that would show him how to do that.

But he was definitely searching for it.

38

"Okay, book fans," said Mr. Lemoncello, smiling into a TV camera in the broadcast booth. "The action inside the Fictionasium is currently more mixed up than the files of Mrs. Basil E. Frankweiler."

"The Lemon Heads have completed their third genre room," reported Dr. Zinchenko. "The Kidzapalooza All-Stars are just now exiting their third room, too."

"Yes," said Mr. Lemoncello. "The All-Stars were slowed down a bit by the surprise appearance of seven samurai, a salami sandwich, slithering snakes, and a sideways sandstorm in their science fiction story. Apparently, the Narrative Drive is stuck in the 'S' section of plot complicators. I was sad to see Kai Kumar leave the game with his GOOHFER card after he was slimed by that sloth. But it certainly was entertaining. The kid knows how to do a pratfall!"

The crowd cheered wildly. They agreed.

"And," said Dr. Zinchenko, "according to this piece of paper I was just handed, you can catch more of Kai's zany antics on a special episode of *Sludge Dodgers* right after this game!"

"How about the Bookworms, Dr. Z? How is our third team faring?"

"Miserably, sir. Four members have already utilized their GOOHFER cards to quit the competition, while team captain Charles Chiltington remains MIM—missing in the maze. We assume he, too, quit. But we don't have confirmation."

"I couldn't find him," said Clarence, the security guard, stepping into the broadcast booth. "I searched underneath all the trapdoors. But then I couldn't get back into the Fictionasium."

"Yes," said Mr. Lemoncello, "apparently the lockdown protocol self-initiated after you left the control booth, Clarence. Ladies and gentlemen, the Fictionasium has become the opposite of a roach motel. You can check out, but you can't check in."

"There's something wrong with the computer!" shouted Mr. Raymo, the head imagineer, who was in the background, shaking his head.

"Well," said Mr. Lemoncello, smiling broadly because he knew he was on live TV, "if you give a mouse a cookie, that's the way it'll crumble."

"What's going on inside the library, Mr. Lemoncello?" shouted Kyle Keeley's father from the front row.

"Must-see TV, if you ask me. With less than an hour to go, millions of viewers are eager to see which team can survive the mash-ups being merrily mixed together by the Narrative Drive supercomputer." Mr. Lemoncello touched his earpiece. "Oh, my. I've just been told that, much like a chimney, our ratings are through the roof!"

"Why were there flying monkeys and Union soldiers in a fairy tale?" shouted Kyle's brother Curtis.

Mr. Lemoncello shrugged. "Artistic license?"

"Who's making this stuff up?"

"A computer with a dazzling and impressive imagination, wouldn't you agree?"

"Wait a minute, Mr. Lemoncello," said Mrs. Keeley. "You're not in control?"

"Nope. But then again, none of us can ever control everything, can we? But it looks like the Lemon Heads, led by your son and brother Kyle, are about to enter their fourth genre: humor!"

"Woo-hoo!" shouted Mike Keeley. "Game on, little bro!"

The whole Keeley family started chanting, "Lem-on Heads! Lem-on Heads!"

"We picked the humor genre specifically for Andrew Peckleman," added Dr. Zinchenko. "He takes everything so seriously. . . ."

"Well," said Mr. Lemoncello, "if the Narrative Drive supercomputer is doing anything remotely close to what we programmed it to do, this next room should be packed with chuckles. Stay tuned and be ready to laugh out loud!"

"Meanwhile," said Dr. Zinchenko, "it looks like the Kidzapalooza All-Stars are poised to enter *their* fourth genre, as well: tall tales."

"The ceiling in that room," added Mr. Lemoncello, "is, of course, ten feet taller than any other room. As for Charles Chiltington? Well, cheer up, folks. I believe in happy endings. I don't think we've heard or seen the last of Mr. Chiltington. He might prove to be this game's breakout star. In fact, I wouldn't be surprised if he ended up giving us all a surprise ending! Because, as someone much wiser than me—the *Goosebumps* movie—once said, 'Every story needs three things: a beginning, a middle, and, most importantly, a twist!' "

39

"Up there," said Kyle, peering through the augmented-reality app on his phone. "See it? It's a big blue mirror."

"It's a fun-house mirror," said Akimi. "It's reflecting us, but we all look distorted and stretched."

"Because," said Sierra, "some books are mirrors, reflecting who we are."

"So, this one must be reflecting who we'd be if we worked at a carnival," said Miguel.

"Or," suggested Sierra, her eyes drifting over to Andrew, "who we could be if we didn't take everything so seriously."

"I look funny," whined Andrew.

"I know," said Akimi.

"Looking funny makes sense," said Kyle, after he'd moved closer to the mirror so he could read what was carved into its frame. "To open our blue lock, we need to go through the humor genre."

"I don't like funny books with poop, underwear, and farts in them," said Andrew. "They are *soooo* immature."

"Must be why we're here, bro," said Miguel. "So far, we've all had to sample our least favorite genre. Comic books for Sierra, sports for me, fairy tales for Akimi, and now humor for you."

"Huh," said Kyle. "That means the fifth room will be for me."

"Let's see, what does Kyle Keeley hate to read?" said Akimi sarcastically. "Oh, just about everything except Lemoncello game instructions."

"That's not true," said Kyle. "I mean, it used to be true, but not since Mr. Lemoncello opened his library and you guys started giving me book suggestions."

"Well," said Andrew, "if this stupid humor room is supposed to be my room, I guess I better be the first one in."

He found the handle and slid the mirror sideways. The rest of the team followed Andrew down a dark tunnel. Kyle brought up the rear. When he slid the mirror shut, a dusty spotlight swung around the dim room until it found a boy who looked exactly like Andrew—except this double wore thick black Groucho glasses complete with fuzzy eyebrows, a rubber nose, and a paintbrush mustache. He was also wearing a natty plaid suit, a bow tie, and floppy clown shoes.

"Say, ANDREW?" said the boy in the spotlight, twirling a bamboo cane.

"Yes?" said Andrew.

"Why did the banana go to the doctor?"

"Bananas don't have doctors. They're fruit. They go to the produce section of the supermarket."

The boy stood there smiling and twirling his cane.

"Play along, Andrew," whispered Akimi. "We need three numbers to open our blue lock before any more poop-hurling monkeys show up."

Andrew sighed. "I give up. Why did the banana go to the doctor?"

"Because," said the Andrew double, "it wasn't peeling well!"

Kyle laughed. Andrew didn't.

"Hey, ANDREW?" said his double. "Did you know my farts are louder than a trombone?"

"No. I did not know that."

"Well, it's true. I learned it last week during band practice. Hey, ANDREW? Know any jokes?"

"Maybe."

"Good. Because you, ANDREW, must now make your audience laugh if your team wants to receive the combination to your blue lock."

That made Kyle nervous. No way could Andrew ever be funny. He thought jokes were stupid and immature.

"We're doomed," muttered Akimi.

"Jokes are stupid and immature!" Andrew shouted.

"You know," said the comedian, "my teacher accused me of being immature once. I told her to get out of my fort."

Andrew had his hands on his hips and a frown on his face.

"Do you know any jokes that are actually funny?" he asked.

"Sure do. But now it's your turn. Make your audience laugh!"

A thick note card popped up from a slot in the floor. Andrew snatched it out of the air.

"What's it say?" asked Sierra.

Andrew read what was printed on the card. " 'Do zombies eat popcorn with their fingers?' "

"No," said Kyle, "they usually eat their fingers first."

Miguel rolled his eyes. Nobody laughed.

"Oh. Okay. Moving on. Joke number two. 'Why did the tomato blush?' "

"I don't know," said Miguel. "Why?"

"Because," said Andrew's holographic double. "Because. Beeee. Causssssse."

He SIZZLE-ZIZZed with static, sputtered into a shower of fuzzy pixels, and disappeared with a POP!

"That's it?" said Andrew. "No punch line?"

"I think we're experiencing another computer glitch," said Miguel.

"The tomato blushed because he saw the salad dressing," said Akimi. "That's, like, so second grade. . . ."

"Well, you guys didn't laugh!" said Andrew. "I guess

185

that means we don't get our fourth lock's combination. This room has been a total and complete—"

"Braaaaains! Must eat braaaaains!"

A horde of foot-dragging zombies lurched out of the shadows.

"Uh-oh," said Akimi. "I think your audience just showed up."

"And your jokes don't have to knock them dead," said Miguel. "Because they already are!"

40

"Kyle?" said Sierra, backing up a few feet as the flesh-dripping mob lurched forward. "Why are there zombies in a humor story?"

"Oh, man," moaned Miguel. "One lame zombie joke just triggered a whole zombie apocalypse!"

"Or somebody's messing with Mr. Lemoncello's story-making software," said Kyle.

Two dozen zombies, their arms extended, staggered around the room.

"Do you know what it takes to become a zombie?" asked the drooling leader of the undead.

"Yeah," said Akimi. "Dead-ication!"

"Ooooooh! Smart! I like a girl with braaaaains!"

The zombies circled the Lemon Heads, who kept backing up until they formed a tight knot in the center of the room.

"I'm scared, Andrew!" shouted Sierra.

"They're just holograms!" said Kyle.

"No!" said Andrew. "They're my audience! If I can make them laugh, we'll get the combination to our fourth lock!"

"Go for it!" shouted Akimi. "Fast."

"Okay." Andrew tugged nervously at the collar of his MoCap suit. "Good afternoon, guys and ghouls. I guess you're here in the humor section because, uh, we can see your funny bones! Heck, we can see all your bones. Well, to be honest, none of us were dying to meet you."

The skeletal zombies stopped lunging forward and looked at Andrew. A bright locomotive beacon of light hit him. He was on!

"So," he said to his undead audience, "do you know where zombie monkeys live?"

"No," chanted the zombies. "Where do zombie monkeys live?"

"In the brain forest!" said Andrew.

The zombies still weren't laughing.

"Excuse me, ma'am," Andrew said to a zombie in the front row of the tattered mob. "Is that your boyfriend?"

The zombie nodded, which made her head nearly jiggle off her spine.

"Sheesh. Where'd you dig him up?"

Finally, the zombies started to chuckle. And then laugh! Soon they were laughing so hard they shook themselves loose and fell into a crumpled, dusty heap of bones and tattered rags.

The spotlight split in two, with one half swinging to a far corner of the room, where it found Andrew's double.

"Hey, ANDREW?"

"Yeah?"

"Good jokes."

Andrew grinned. "Thanks, pal."

"You ready for my big, boffo closer?"

"Sure."

"Why was six afraid of seven?"

"Easy," said Andrew. "Because seven eight nine."

"Woo-hoo!" shouted Kyle. "That's it. The combination for lock number four: seven, eight, nine."

He rolled the wheels on the blinking blue suitcase lock to those three numbers and pulled it open.

"Oh, yeah!" said the big voice in the ceiling as holograms of unspooling toilet paper rolls arced through the room. "Lock four? Open! One more? Breakout!"

"Way to go, Andrew!" shouted Miguel.

"Thank you," said Andrew. "You know what, guys?"

"What?" said Sierra.

"It's fun to be funny! Safe, too. Because zombies never eat clowns. You know why?"

"Why?" said his teammates.

"Because they taste funny. Now let's make like a banana and split!"

The Lemon Heads hurried out of the Humor Room.

In the control room, Charles watched them exit.

Okay, he thought. *That didn't work.*

The zombie horde hadn't scared off Keeley's team, and so far, his attack on the Kidzapalooza team had only sent one player, Kai Kumar, heading for the exits.

Charles flipped through more manuals.

"There's no way to send holograms into the hallways," he muttered.

But . . .

He might be able to send one of the robotic dummies into the maze. But there were only a limited number available: some hair-snagging bat drones, a wrinkled old fairy-tale king, an angry slab-of-granite gargoyle . . .

Charles rechecked the monitors.

The Kidzapalooza All-Stars were having trouble in their Tall Tale Room, trying to help Pecos Bill lasso a tornado. Gabrielle Grande insisted on being the one to twirl the rope, a real prop.

"You've missed like eighteen times," said Jaylen. "Let someone else give it a shot, girl."

"Like me," said Peyton. "After all, Action is my middle name."

"Only because stunt doubles do all your dangerous action sequences for you!" shouted Gabrielle.

"Hey," said Haley, trying her perky best to lighten the mood, "how about I give it a whirl?"

"Fine. Whatevs."

Haley grabbed the rope, got it spinning, and tossed it at the strobing target.

"Not bad, little missy," said Pecos Bill as Haley snared the holographic tornado's tail on her first fling. "Was you raised by coyotes, too?"

"Probably," said Gabrielle snidely. "It's why she dresses like that."

"Hey, hey, hey," said Haley, ignoring the insult. "Have we earned our puzzle?"

"You betcha!" said Pecos Bill. "Y'all got you a four-digit lock there?"

"Yep!" said Jaylen.

"Then I reckon you better do the math!"

A holographic math puzzle hovered in the air in front of the four Kidzapalooza stars:

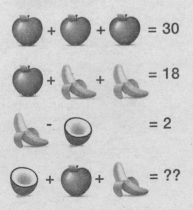

From his viewing post at the computer console, Charles could hardly stand to see what was about to happen. If the Kidzapalooza All-Stars solved the puzzle, they'd earn the combination to their fourth lock—just like Keeley's team had.

All his enemies would be tied for the lead.

And one lock away from breaking out of the library!

41

"Losing is not an option!" Charles said out loud, since nobody could hear him in the control room.

He dragged the Tall Tale Room screen into the Active Story Window and scrolled through the "plot complicator" options until he found the "plague" category.

He poised his finger over the command key.

He tapped the button.

A dark swarm of bees blocked out the light in the room.

"Shoo, doggies," said Pecos Bill. "I ain't seen that many bees since I picked up a dictionary and flipped to the second letter."

"I hate bees!" shouted Jaylen, and started doing a flurry of dab moves to dodge the buzzing cluster.

"They're not real bees, dude!" shouted Peyton.

"I don't care. They look real!"

Jaylen slipped his GOOHFER card into a slot and dropped out of the game.

"Yes!" said Charles, enjoying the fruits of his labor. "Another one bites the dust!"

"Peyton?" squealed Gabrielle, swatting at the buzzing swarm. "Do something!"

"To the max, babe!" He looked at all the bees. "Any suggestions?"

"Yes," said Haley. "How about we solve the puzzle and get out of here?"

She cleared away the cloud of computer-generated bees circling her head so she could focus on the puzzle.

"Okay," said Haley. "Three apples equal thirty."

"So, one equals ten!" said Peyton.

"How can one equal ten?" shouted Gabrielle.

Haley ignored her. "Ten plus two bananas equals eighteen."

"Awesome!" said Peyton. "So, one equals four."

"Oh, great," said Gabrielle. "Now one equals four? I thought it equaled ten."

"Banana minus coconut equals two," said Haley.

"So, coconut equals two!" said Peyton.

Gabrielle rolled her eyes. "You guys need new math tutors. Seriously, you do."

Peyton and Haley ignored her. Again.

"Making the final number . . . ," said Haley.

Peyton took over. "Two plus ten plus four equals—"

"Sixteen!" they said together, and slapped a high five.

"Did you guys just squish a bee?" asked Gabrielle.

"Nope," said Haley. "We just figured out the combination to our fourth lock: thirty, eighteen, two, *sixteen*!"

They quickly spun the dials on their blinking four-digit lock and removed it from the codex.

"Oh, yeah!" bellowed the video game voice. "Fourth lock? Open! One more? Breakout!"

"Booyah!" said Peyton. "Way to be incredible to the max, Haley!"

Gabrielle narrowed her eyes and shot icicles at Haley.

Back in the control room, Charles's phone buzzed.

His hand trembled as he read what his father had to say this time.

> Where are you?
> There are only forty-eight minutes left in the game.

Charles looked back at the screens.

Both teams were heading for the hallways.

They each only needed to go through one more room and open one more lock.

It was time to send in one of the audio-animatronic dummies.

Charles picked the meanest, ugliest, and nastiest one.

The one that couldn't be stopped because it was made out of stone.

The snarling gargoyle.

42

As soon as Kyle and his teammates bumped into the Kid-zapalooza All-Stars in the narrow corridors of the Fiction-asium's maze, he noticed the one lock still dangling off the clasp of their codex.

"You guys need yellow, too?"

"That's right," said Gabrielle.

"What happened to the rest of your team?" asked Akimi.

"We lost Kai and Jaylen," said Peyton, doing his best to sound like a choked-up action hero. "But we're TV stars. We cope. We adjust. We play on."

All the players still in the game had their phones up, searching the nearby walls.

"I only see one yellow window," reported Miguel.

"Same here," said Haley.

"Where are the Bookworms?" asked Sierra, looking up

at the flat-screen monitor with the mosaic of images from the game. All cameras were focused on the eight players facing off in the labyrinth.

"Did Charles quit?" Kyle wondered aloud.

"You guys?" said Miguel. "There's only forty-six minutes left in the game."

"So, who on your team needs yellow?" asked Akimi.

"What do you mean?" said Gabrielle.

"So far," explained Miguel, "every genre we've been in was chosen because it was one of our players' least favorite kind of story."

"Yellow is going to be for me," said Kyle.

Both yellow locks on the two codexes started blinking.

Kyle moved closer to the window and read what was written on its frame. "Huh. Realistic fiction. Wonder why I need that?"

"Who goes first?" demanded Gabrielle.

"Do you want to rock-paper-scissors for it?" asked Kyle.

"Fine." Gabrielle balled up her right hand into a fist and rested it on the palm of her left hand.

Kyle mirrored her moves. "On three."

"One, two, three!" said Gabrielle.

She shot out a flat hand for "paper." Kyle shot out two fingers for "scissors."

"Scissors cuts paper!" said Akimi. "Boom! Kyle wins!"

"Okay," said Kyle. "We'll go in first and—"

A tremendous growl echoed up the corridor. It was

followed by what sounded like somebody rolling a sack of cinder blocks.

Suddenly, a squat granite gargoyle sculpted to resemble a snarling goblin tumbled into view.

"It's an out-of-control bowling ball!" shouted Miguel.

"Retreat!" shouted Andrew. "Retreat!"

The eight players raced up the winding hallways.

The gargoyle raced after them.

The players found themselves backed up against a wall with no exit, only a control panel. They were trapped in a dead end. The gargoyle was only twenty feet away.

"We're all going to die!" shrieked Peyton. "That thing's not a hologram. It's real!"

He started fumbling for his GOOHFER card.

Gabrielle slapped his hand. "Get a grip, Peyton. You can't quit! You're Peyton McCallister!"

"Not if I'm dead!"

He slipped his card into the slot and dropped out of the game.

The gargoyle snorted and pawed its clawed feet against the carpeted floor.

Kyle had an idea. He turned to Haley.

"Shoot for it again? On three?"

"You got it," said Haley.

The gargoyle lunged forward.

Kyle and Haley pounded their fists into their palms.

"One . . ."

The gargoyle rolled into a somersault to become a rumbling boulder.

"Two!"

The massive stone picked up speed.

"Three!"

Kyle and Haley both shot out flat hands.

The gargoyle skidded to a halt.

It grumbled a little, but it knew the rules of the game.

Paper covers rock.

Paper wins.

"Good game," the gargoyle grunted. "Gotta roll. They need me back in gothic horror."

"So long, Rock Butt!" said Gabrielle.

The gargoyle hobbled away. Haley and Kyle fist-bumped.

"Go, Buckeyes," said Haley with a wink.

"Always," said Kyle.

"Hey, you guys," said Akimi. "Check this out."

She pointed at the two keyholes she'd just noticed underneath the slot on the box where Peyton had inserted his GOOHFER card.

"According to what I heard Mr. Raymo telling Mr. Lemoncello, that's how you alter the story in any Fiction-asium room," said Miguel. "The key holes are on all the GOOHFER boxes. But you need *two* keys!"

"Which we don't have," said Kyle.

"We also don't have much more time," said Akimi.

"That little stunt with the rolling gargoyle cost us three whole minutes."

"Come on!" said Kyle, sprinting back up the hall. The others followed him.

When they reached the video screen near the yellow window, it was no longer a grid of multiple camera angles.

It was just a big digital clock.

00:42:58

There were only forty-two minutes and fifty-eight seconds left in the game.

43

"Okay, game boys and girls," said Mr. Lemoncello, narrating the action in the maze from his post in the broadcast booth. "Kyle Keeley is leading his team through the yellow window."

The crowd cheered.

"But Haley and Gabrielle, the two remaining Kidzapalooza All-Stars, will be crawling in right behind them," added Dr. Zinchenko.

"We love you, Gabby!" shouted a fan holding up a sign.

"This thing is neck and neck!" said Mr. Lemoncello. "Just like a giraffe convention. Any idea where that gargoyle came from?"

"It's a glitch in the system!" shouted Mr. Raymo, who was pacing in the background, tugging at the tufts of hair ringing his otherwise bald head. "The Narrative Drive is programmed to maximize plot twists. It might keep randomly adding unexpected elements!"

"What fun!" said Mr. Lemoncello. "There are, of course, only two teams left. The Lemon Heads and the seriously diminished Kidzapalooza All-Stars. All the players on the Bookworms team bailed out earlier and nobody knows where their captain courageous, Charles Chiltington, might be."

"Sir?" said Clarence, the security guard, stepping into the booth and handing Mr. Lemoncello a walkie-talkie. "It's for you."

"Hang on, folks." Mr. Lemoncello took the radio from Clarence. "Let's see who this is! Yello? This is Luigi Lemoncello."

"It's me, sir," said a voice. "Charles Chiltington."

"Charles!" gasped Mr. Lemoncello. "Charles Chiltington?"

"Yes, sir."

"Where are you, my dear boy? We've all been so worried about you! We thought you were trapped under the floor wrestling with an undulating whoopee cushion!"

"I'm fine, sir."

"Thank heavens! Can you tell us your current location?"

"In the control room with the Narrative Drive supercomputer."

"Get out of there!" shouted Mr. Raymo in the background. "The computer is on the fritz!"

"Charles?" Mr. Lemoncello calmly said into the walkie-talkie.

"Yes, sir?"

"What, exactly, are you doing in the Narrative Drive supercomputer control room?"

"Well, sir, I don't mean to be a tattletale, but it seems your security guard—I believe his name is Clarence—deserted his post."

"No!" said Mr. Lemoncello, sounding horrified (even though he shot Clarence a wink).

"Yes, sir," said Charles. "He must've pushed the wrong buttons before he left. That's why all the weird stuff like zombies and bee swarms and rolling gargoyles started popping up. I've been in here trying to fix it for over an hour!"

"Charles, the Kidzapalooza Network and I can't thank you enough. You saved the game. Now, if you will kindly override the lockdown, Dr. Zinchenko and I will come inside and, with the twist of our twin keys, rewrite the room scenarios back to their original settings."

"I, uh, can't find the unlock button, sir. And if it's okay with you, I'd like to leave the control room and finish opening the locks on my codex. I want to win this game, sir!"

"Really? You only have forty-two minutes to complete three rooms, Charles."

"I know. It won't be easy. But you're the one who so wisely taught me a very valuable and important lesson: The game's not over until it's over."

"Charles?"

"Yes, sir?"

"Thank you for all you have done today. Good luck on your journey."

"Thank you, sir. See you outside at the finish line. I intend to break out first, win this game, and make my father proud. My mother, too, of course."

"Of course. We're all pulling for you, Charles. More than you may ever know!"

44

Take notes! Charles told himself. *Look up all the answers before you leave.*

He quickly scrolled through the story outlines for his three remaining genres: historical fiction, poetry, and mythology.

This would be better than a cheat guide to a video game. It'd be more like having the teacher's answer key for a final exam!

This would guarantee his victory!

He worked backward on his computer.

Mythology. Poetry. Historical fiction.

After finding what he needed, Charles raced to the Historical Fiction Room, where mighty cannon blasts still rumbled and the air smelled like gunpowder, campfire smoke, and freshly flung mud.

Charles plucked up all nine concealed prop pieces from their hiding places in less than thirty seconds.

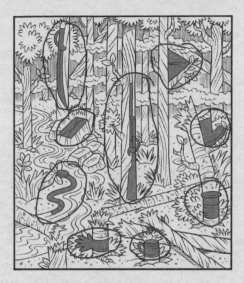

When he was done, the holographic Abraham Lincoln reappeared to give him a riddle.

"Four score and seven years ago . . ."

"The combination is seventeen seventy-six!" exclaimed Charles, working the wheel before Lincoln was finished. "One, seven, seven, six. Thanks, Abe!"

The flashing golden lock popped open. A sea of small holographic American flags waved in the air.

"Oh, yeah!" boomed the deep voice. "Third lock? Open! Two more? Breakout!"

Charles dashed out of the Historical Fiction Room and

into the hall, where he quickly found a robin's-egg-blue window.

"Poetry!" said Charles.

He clambered through the window and entered a dark and moody room. A hologram of the famous poet Robert Frost stepped out of the shadows. Two roads, cluttered with fallen leaves, appeared on the floor.

"Two roads diverged in a yellow wood—"

"I'll take the one on the left, Bob," interrupted Charles.

He hurried up the leaf-strewn path and bumped into another hologram. This one, Charles knew, was Kwame Alexander, Newbery Medal–winning author of *The Crossover*, a novel in verse.

"Please recite the world's shortest poem," said the holographic poet.

"No problem," said Charles. "Fleas. Adam. Had 'em."

"Swish!" said Kwame Alexander. "Solve this final puzzle and you'll score the moves you need to open your next lock!"

An image of nine basketballs appeared in the center of the room.

"Move any two basketballs, CHARLES," said the poet, "and, if you dare, form a square."

"Easy, sir," said Charles (because, of course, he'd already seen the answer).

He touched one ball and slid it down and toward the right. The second ball he slid down and to the left.

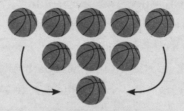

With just two moves, he'd formed a square.

He'd also learned the combination to his fourth lock, which was a directional lock.

"Down, right, down, left."

The robin's-egg-blue lock blinked and snapped open. Holograms of different words that all meant "congratulations" wafted around the room like confetti.

"Oh, yeah," Charles said along with the video game voice. "Fourth lock? Open! One more? Breakout!"

And the game was officially tied. On the nearest monitor, he could hear the amazed audience cheering for him.

"Char-les! Chil-ting-ton!"

Winning felt amazing!

Charles only had one more room to go. Mythology.

He raced out of the Poetry Room, made a few sharp turns, and found what he was looking for: a marble door that matched the swirly marble-colored lock on his codex. (It looked like a little illuminated bowling ball.)

Charles shoved the door open. He heard stone grind against stone. He stepped through the jagged opening and found himself in a fiery world filled with billowing black smoke and hot blasts of flames leaping up from gas jets.

Charles raised an arm to shield himself from the heat and preprogrammed flare-ups.

"Welcome, CHARLES!" roared a voice in the ceiling. "Proceed to Mount Olympus and use the lightning-bolt blaster to battle Typhocus, the volcanic giant, whom you might remember from *Percy Jackson's Greek Gods*."

Charles noticed a video arcade blaster mounted on a pedestal atop a piece of foam sculpted to look like a craggy mountain.

His phone buzzed in his pocket. Again.

Roiling flames *WHOOSH*ed up all around him and erupted into dramatic fireballs. Charles dug his phone out of his pocket and waited for another fireball eruption to block the cameras before he read what was written on the screen.

> You're doing great!
> Time to hurl lightning bolts.

Charles tucked the phone back into a pocket as the smoke cleared, and he climbed to the summit.

From the peak, he looked down on a hologram of a multiheaded winged dragon that kept vomiting up steady streams of fire.

"I shall lay siege to Mount Olympus!" the monster bellowed.

Charles squeezed the trigger on the blaster.

A lightning bolt ZIZZed out of the nozzle of the rifle.

It hit the floor and erupted into a shower of sparks. It also left smoldering black singe marks.

In other words, it was real.

Why did Mr. Lemoncello put a weapon capable of doing actual damage into this particular room?

Charles tilted up the lightning-bolt blaster and aimed it at the far wall.

He squeezed the trigger.

The rifle ZIZZed again.

And, like a misguided laser, scorched a hole through the wall.

A sudden vibration made him jump.

He dropped down behind the pointy tip of the Mount

210

Olympus set so he could read what his father was texting him without the TV cameras reading it, too.

> Well done, son.

Charles quickly thumbed in a reply.

> What next?

He didn't have to wait long for his answer:

> Finish what your mother started.
> Show everybody how dangerous Mr. Lemoncello's library can be.

45

"Okay," said Kyle, looking up at the monitor in the Realistic Fiction Room. "That is one hundred percent unbelievable."

The live broadcast was showing a slow-motion instant replay of Charles Chiltington clearing both his historical fiction and poetry genres in record time.

The camera cut to crowd reactions.

"No way," said Kyle's brother Mike.

"Impossible," said Charles's former teammate Morgan.

"You're making me very, very proud, Charles!" cheered his mother. "You're the only good and decent thing inside that ridiculous library!"

"Opinions expressed by the crowd are purely their own," said Mr. Lemoncello when the camera switched back to him. "But we are all still mightily impressed. Charles Chiltington is chugging through his rooms and locks like the little engine that could. Why, it's almost as if he knew the answers before he entered the rooms! And now he just has to break out of his final room before the other two teams do! But first, a word from our sponsor. Me!"

The live feed cut to a commercial.

"Yo, check it out," said Miguel as the lights came up in the Realistic Fiction Room to reveal cafeteria tables similar to the ones at Alexandriaville Middle School.

"There's scripts," said Akimi, moving over to one of the tables. "With our names on them."

"I hope I got a funny part," said Andrew.

"There's scripts here for Haley and Gabrielle, too!" said Sierra. "I guess we really are playing this room together."

"Where's mine?" asked Kyle.

"I dunno," said Miguel. "Maybe over there."

He pointed to a table off in a far corner of the room. There was a thin stack of papers on it. Kyle hurried over to it. Charles had moved on to his fifth room. They were all tied. There was no time to waste.

Haley and Gabrielle tumbled into the room.

"We're in a commercial break," said Gabrielle. "Go ask your rube friends what we're supposed to do! Hurry! Scoot! I need to touch up my nail polish for when I win."

Haley raced over to Kyle's table.

"Hey," she said.

"Hey," said Kyle. "Can I ask you a question?"

"Maybe."

"Is Gabrielle Grande always that mean?"

Haley looked around to make sure nobody could hear what she said next. "It's complicated. Gabby thinks I'm a threat. She's been a Kidzapalooza star for so long. Then I came along. I sort of feel bad for her. . . ."

"Well, we're all super proud of *you*," said Kyle. "When I see you on TV, I'm like, wow. You don't even seem like a real person."

"I guess the Haley on TV is like a character in a book. She isn't really real. It's a job, Kyle. One I need and actually love. If my team wins this game . . ."

"You might get to star in your own game show on Kidzapalooza."

"Yeah."

"Haley?" shouted Gabrielle, waving her fingertips to dry her nails. "Get over here!"

"Talk to you later, Kyle."

Haley ran back to join Gabrielle.

Kyle checked the game clock. They still had thirty-two minutes.

The commercials ended and the live-feed screen showed Charles on top of Mount Olympus, firing lightning bolts at a lava-spewing monster.

Kyle picked up the script with his name printed on its cover.

When he did, projectors turned the blank black walls into the walls of a middle school cafeteria, complete with video of kids shuffling through the food line and cafeteria workers with hairnets dishing out mystery meat, greasy chicken tenders, and soggy slices of cheese pizza. The smell-a-vision system was working overtime.

"You guys?" Kyle called out. "If we want to beat Charles Chiltington, we need to get busy! He's setting indoor gaming speed records."

"But wait a second," said Miguel. "How do we defeat, you know, these other guys?" He held one hand sideways to shield the finger he was pointing at Haley and Gabrielle.

"Mr. Lemoncello?" Akimi said to the nearest camera. "Dr. Zinchenko? How can we win if we have to play this room with a team of rivals?"

There was no reply.

"You guys?" said Haley. "The clock is ticking. So why don't we just start playing and worry about winners and losers later?"

"Ha!" scoffed Gabrielle. "I think we already know who the losers are!" She pointed at Kyle and his friends.

"Let's just play on," said Kyle, who had to shout because he was so far away. "This script will probably lead us to a puzzle or a riddle. Whoever solves *it* first will get the key to open their *yellow lock* first."

"Okay," said Gabrielle. "I, of course, have the first lines, because Mr. Lemoncello knows I'm the kind of star that can pull in big ratings, no matter the material."

"So, read your lines!" said Miguel.

"Look at him," Gabrielle read (extremely dramatically). "Sitting over there like he's better than us."

"Who does Miles Millerson think he is?" added Akimi, reading her part.

The live feed cut to the Realistic Fiction Room.

Akimi, Miguel, Sierra, and Andrew had been electronically recostumed, their MoCap suits becoming very familiar clothing: exactly what they'd worn to school on Friday.

"Dudes?" said Miguel, standing up like the script instructed him to. He raised an arm to point at Kyle sitting off in the distance. "I officially hate that guy."

A camera pushed in for a close-up of Kyle, who glanced up at the nearest video monitor.

Thanks to the digital effects, it looked like he was wearing a navy-blue blazer, a starched button-down dress shirt, a striped tie, and khaki slacks.

In other words, Kyle Keeley looked exactly like Charles Chiltington!

46

Come on, thought Kyle, who hadn't worn a blue blazer once in his entire life, not even on Mother's Day or Easter. *I look ridiculous!*

But they needed to open their last lock. They needed to solve some sort of riddle to earn its key.

So he needed to stay focused and play out the realistic fiction scene.

"I hate Miles Millerson," he heard Andrew read from his script.

"So?" read Gabrielle. "Everybody hates Millerson."

"Not my parents," read Miguel. "They wish I could be more like him."

"He's such a suck-up," said Akimi.

"He's a jerk," said Miguel, pointing at Kyle at his distant table. "That's why he always sits there all by himself."

"Well," read Sierra, "maybe there's a reason Miles acts the way he does."

"Definitely," replied Andrew. "His jerkiness combined with his jerkitude and jerkosity."

"Um, you guys?" Kyle cried out. "I'm sitting right here."

"Yo," coached Miguel. "You're not you. You're this Miles Millerson character. Stick to the script, bro."

"Yeah," whined Gabrielle, who'd skipped ahead in the script and discovered a pile of blank pages. "At least you have lines coming up. We just have to sit here and basically do nothing. I need to talk to my agent about this. . . ."

Kyle shook his head. Of all the rooms they'd worked through, this one was the most ridiculous. It was also taking up a lot of time. The clock was down to twenty-nine minutes.

"Miles Millerson's family is so rich," read Andrew.

"How rich are they?" asked Haley.

"Why, they're so rich," read Andrew, "their boogers are greasy green emeralds."

A holographic teacher appeared near Kyle's table.

"Hello, Miles," she said.

Then she stood there. Waiting. Blinking.

Kyle realized it was probably his turn to say something.

He glanced down at his script and reluctantly read what was written there.

"Why, good afternoon, Ms. Langan. My, you certainly

look fetching in that cardigan sweater. I love the kitty cats embroidered on the pockets. Did you knit it yourself?"

"Yes, Miles. I did."

"I am honored to have you as my teacher, Ms. Langan. You are both artsy *and* crafty!"

"Well, aren't you sweet? Enjoy your lunch, Miles. I wish all my students were as polite as you."

"Then they wouldn't have any friends, either," Kyle ad-libbed.

The teacher hologram started blinking again. "Pardon? I did not understand that. Please repeat your remark."

Kyle went back to his script. "Thank you, Ms. Langan. That is kindly, considerate, and benevolent of you to say."

The 3-D teacher image smiled. "My, what a marvelous vocabulary you possess, Miles. I imagine your parents must be very proud of you. So very, very *proud-d-d-d*."

Her voice stuttered and echoed on the last "PROUD."

As the word boomed around the room and rang in Kyle's ears, the lights blacked out. The video walls vanished. The room was plunged into total darkness.

"What the . . ."

Kyle stood up. He heard the *WHOOSH* of a sliding panel and the rumble of caster wheels.

Next came the faint and muffled voices of his friends and competitors from behind a thick, sound-deadening wall.

A single, dusty shaft of light thumped on. It sliced through the velvety blackness like a bright knife.

Kyle looked around. His cafeteria table was gone. So was his script. So were all the other players.

The sound of crisp and steady footfalls echoed in the darkness.

"You guys?" Kyle called out.

No one answered.

He felt an icy wind bite into his face. He smelled fear (his own, not from smell-a-vision).

A new holographic character strode into the sharply angled light cutting across the blackness.

It was a tall man with a pinched face and wire-rimmed glasses. He wore a navy-blue blazer, a crisply pressed white shirt, a striped tie, khaki pants, and shiny loafers.

"It's time we had a chat, Miles," said the angry man.

"Um, okay," said Kyle.

"You need to stay focused on winning this game."

"I'm, uh, trying. . . ."

"Good," said the man, his lips curling up into an evil smile. "Because Millersons never lose!"

47

Kyle quickly realized what was going on.

This was the Realistic Fiction Room. That meant he was inside a made-up story based on stuff that was mostly true. He was experiencing what life might be like if he were Charles Chiltington!

"Don't worry," said the holographic Mr. Millerson. "No one can see us."

He pointed toward the walls, which quickly illuminated, one section after another, until the light had completed a full circuit of the room.

"There are no cameras. No microphones. No live feed of the broadcast. Not even a countdown clock. It's just you and me, Miles."

"Okay," said Kyle. "That's a pretty goofy thing to do for a TV show. . . ."

The stern figure ignored him and said what he'd been programmed to say.

"Winning isn't everything, son. It's the only thing! Tell me, Miles—do you want to be a winner?"

Kyle shrugged. "Usually."

"I beg your pardon?"

"Usually I like to win. I'm supercompetitive."

"Good for you, son! *Nos vincere semper!*"

"Um, is that Latin?"

"Of course it is!"

"Well, sir, I study Spanish at school, not Latin. *¿Donde está la biblioteca? La biblioteca está aquí.*"

"*Nos vincere semper* means 'We always win!' It's our Millerson family motto. When you don't win, you disappoint me and every Millerson who has ever lived. Do I make myself clear?"

Glowing words appeared on the black wall behind the frightful figure. Kyle's new script.

"Yes, Father," read Kyle. "I understand."

And, suddenly, Kyle did.

He totally understood Charles Chiltington. He still didn't like him. But he understood why he acted the way he did.

"And now," said the imaginary Mr. Millerson, "I suppose you'll be wanting these."

He pointed to the floor with a bony finger.

A pinpoint spotlight widened into a tiny circle of light on the floor.

It ringed two yellow keys.

222

One for the yellow lock on his team's codex, one for the yellow lock on the other team's.

"Trust me, son," said Mr. Millerson. "Those are the only two yellow keys in this room. Therefore, you are now at a distinct advantage over your competition."

Mr. Millerson smiled.

He seemed to be growing even more evil.

A stench of death—like hamburger meat in a foam cooler without any ice—wafted through the dark room.

"Remember, Miles, no one can see us. Mr. Lemoncello is too focused on that other boy who wishes to defeat you. Charles, I believe?"

"Yeah. He's been my nemesis since forever."

"You wouldn't mind beating him again, would you?"

"No, sir."

"Good, good. You know what you need to do with those two keys on the floor."

"What exactly is that, sir?"

"Simple. Win with one. Forget you ever found the other."

48

Heavy thunder seemed to rumble through the walls.

Kyle turned around to see what was going on.

The wall dividing the Realistic Fiction Room in half *WHOOSH*ed back open. The holographic Mr. Millerson vanished.

"Are you seeing this?" asked Akimi as Kyle hurried back into the section of the room with video monitors. The other players were staring up at the screens displaying what people tuned in to the Kidzapalooza Network saw on *their* TVs.

Charles Chiltington standing at the summit of Mount Olympus hurling lightning bolts at the walls.

"He only had one lock left but he's decided to trash the place instead of going for his final puzzle!" shouted Miguel.

Charles fired another lightning bolt.

The TV screens whited out.

"And now another word from our sponsor," said the announcer. "Friends? Do you have enough insurance, should disaster hurl a lightning bolt at your family's plans?"

"We need to stop him," said Akimi.

"But how can we make Charles stop trying to destroy the library?" asked Sierra. "It's been his obsession ever since he lost the first escape game."

Kyle fidgeted with the two yellow keys he'd hidden in the hip pocket of his MoCap suit.

"He's not all bad," said Kyle.

"Wha-hut?" said Akimi. "He's blowing up the Fiction-asium!"

"He's showing the world how dangerous a freewheeling library like Mr. Lemoncello's can be," said Andrew, who used to hang out with Charles on a semi-regular basis. "It's what his mother's always wanted him to do."

"I think this is more about his father," said Kyle.

"What makes you say that?" asked Gabrielle. "Are you some kind of child psychologist?"

Kyle pointed at the open wall. "When that thing slid shut, let's just say I walked a mile or two in Charles's shoes. I think I know why he acts the way he does. I also think I know how to open up our yellow lock."

He pulled one yellow key out of his pocket.

"You found our final key?" exclaimed Miguel. "Woo-hoo! Awesome."

Andrew turned to Haley and Gabrielle. "I guess this is the part where we shake hands and congratulate you on a

225

good game because, apparently, we just won and you just lost."

"Nobody's losing," said Kyle.

Out came the second yellow key.

"Here you go," said Kyle, tossing it to Haley.

"You found their key, too?" said Akimi.

"Yeah."

"And you're just giving it to them?"

Kyle shrugged. "Some things are more important than winning."

Akimi stared at him. "Who are you and what have you done with my friend Kyle Keeley?"

Kyle laughed. "I'm hoping there's something in one of these two locked codexes that'll help us change Charles's mind about destroying the library. Come on. We need to hurry."

Both teams inserted their yellow keys into their yellow locks.

The keys worked. Indoor fireworks exploded. Balloons dropped from the ceiling. *Real* balloons.

"Oh, yeah!" boomed the video game voice. "Final locks? Open! It's breakout time!"

Kyle pulled the blinking yellow lock out of its clasp. Haley did the same thing with hers.

They both pried open their heavy codex covers. Inside the pages of each oversized book was a hollowed-out rectangle.

"It's like one of those book safes!" said Andrew.

Tucked into each nook was an old-fashioned scrolled

key shaped like an L. Microchips were embedded in their teeth.

"It's a control key," said Miguel. "For the Fiction-asium. Mr. Lemoncello has one. Mr. Raymo, the head imagineer, too. If you put two keys into any of the control boxes spread throughout the Fictionasium and simulta-neously twist them to the right, you can reprogram the action in the nearest room."

"The keys might also work on the bank vault door," said Andrew.

The far wall of the Realistic Fiction Room slid open.

The maze had worked its way around the Rotunda Reading Room and back to the lobby of the library. The bank vault door was less than thirty feet away, just beyond the gurgling fountain of Mr. Lemoncello.

Gabrielle snatched the L-shaped key out of Haley's hand.

"Wait!" shouted Haley.

"No thank you, Haley!" laughed Gabrielle. "Waiting is for wannabes like you, not breakout stars like me!" She dashed to the door and jabbed the key into one of the two side-by-side slots. "Yes! It fits!"

She twisted the key.

Nothing clicked.

She pushed on the door. She pulled on it.

Nothing.

"The dumb door is busted!" she said. "It won't budge."

"Because," said Kyle, pointing at the empty second keyhole, "you need two keys."

"What?" said Gabrielle. "We can't win alone?"

"Of course not," said Sierra, gesturing at the motto inscribed on the base of the Lemoncello fountain. " 'Knowledge not shared remains unknown.' "

"Guess the same thing is true about keys," said Akimi. "If they're not shared, someone's always locked out."

Gabrielle thrust out her hand to Kyle. "Give me yours."

"Um, why?"

"Because if you help me win, you can be on my show. You know—as an extra in the background. You can hold my coat or something."

"No thanks."

"Haley?" Gabrielle huffed. "Do something!"

The walls shook again.

"I will," said Haley. "What I'm going to do is help Kyle and his team stop Charles from destroying the library."

"Fine. Whatevs," said Gabrielle. "But I'm a star. I don't do 'group activities.' Text me when you guys are done so we can break out already. I need to go find a snack." Gabrielle tossed the L-shaped key back to Haley. "Have fun with your lame-o friends from nowheresville."

She sashayed out of the room.

"Huh," said Akimi, smiling at Haley. "It's us against Charles. Again."

"Actually," said Andrew, "in the escape game—"

"You were disqualified," said Miguel. "We know, we know."

"But we're glad you're on our team now," said Sierra.

"Thanks."

The closest video screen flashed white.

Charles was still hurling lightning bolts at the walls of the Mythology Room.

"Hey, hey, you guys," said Haley, pumping up her perkiness (because she knew she was still on camera). "How do we stop Charles from doing permanent damage to this library's permanent collection?"

"Use these two keys to open the front door," said Miguel. "Then the cops could bust in and arrest him."

Kyle turned to Miguel. "You said a pair of 'L' keys can reprogram the Fictionasium rooms, correct?"

"That's right," said Miguel.

"Okay. So, instead of breaking out of the library, how about we help Charles break out of his jerkiness and jerkosity first?"

"Wha-hut?" said Akimi. "Have you been watching *Dr. Phil*?"

Kyle ignored her.

"We have two keys. That means we can reprogram that room he's in. We just need to think up a good story. One that convinces Charles to do what he knows, deep down, is right."

"Works for me," said Haley. "I like happy endings."

"Fine," said Akimi, "but it better be a *short* story. We only have nineteen more minutes before the game's officially over!"

49

A thundering blast made the maze partition on their left rumble.

It was like being in one movie theater of a multiplex and hearing the reverberating boom of explosions from the disaster movie playing in the theater next door.

"Charles is behind that wall!" said Kyle.

"That's got to be the Mythology Room," said Sierra.

"You guys," said Miguel, standing next to a control box mounted on a sleek pedestal. "This looks like the unit for mythology. Those are the key slots to override the pre-programmed story sequence."

Kyle checked out the miniature tablet computer docked at the top of the box. He figured that was where the story options would come up once he and Haley inserted their two keys and gave them a simultaneous twist to the right.

Kyle heard another *BA-BOOM* and the floor quaked.

"Whoa," said Akimi. "He's really whaling on that lightning-bolt blaster." She pointed to another one of those security-style video screens split into eight different image boxes. Kyle could see Charles firing random blasts of jagged white light.

"Check it out," said Miguel, pointing to the image in the lower right-hand corner of the screen. It was the video feed from a camera in the Rotunda Reading Room. Every time Charles shot a lightning bolt, the books on the fiction wall wobbled. "If somebody doesn't stop him, Charles might do some serious damage to the main library."

Mr. Lemoncello and Dr. Zinchenko appeared on a square in the middle of the eight-image display. They were in the broadcast booth. A rectangular clock with red digits was counting down the time remaining in the game.

00:18:24

"Charles?" said Mr. Lemoncello. "I'm begging you. Please do not destroy my library on national TV."

"What?" shouted Charles. "How can you see what I'm doing in here? I thought I blew up the camera for this room!"

"Oh, I guess I'm just three times lucky. I also have backups for my backups."

231

"This library is a dangerous place!" shouted Charles. "My mother always said so! Dangerous books. Dangerous games. Dangerous lightning-bolt blasters."

"But you could still win the game, Charles," said Mr. Lemoncello.

"What?"

"You can still win. It seems that the other two teams have hit a dead end, even though they're nowhere near Norvelt."

Charles stopped firing lightning bolts. "Seriously?"

"Most indubitably," said Mr. Lemoncello, using one of Charles's favorite words. "Look at the video monitor. The Lemon Heads and Haley Daley are in a hallway gawking at a TV screen. Gabrielle Grande is off taking a snack break."

Kyle, Akimi, Miguel, Sierra, and Andrew waved at the nearest TV camera. So did Haley Daley.

"Oh, it's them against me again, huh?" said Charles.

"Yes, Charles," said Mr. Lemoncello. "But I think you can do this. . . ."

Charles loosened his grip on the lightning-bolt blaster.

Kyle turned to Haley. "You ready?"

Haley nodded. She and Kyle both inserted their L-shaped keys into the control box.

"On three," said Kyle.

"One, two, three," said Haley.

They twisted both keys hard to the right.

A list of story options appeared on the tablet computer. Kyle used his finger to scroll through them.

He found the character he was looking for and tapped in a series of commands.

Charles Chiltington was about to meet an unexpected visitor in the Mythology Room.

50

"All right!" shouted Charles. "You've got a deal, Mr. Lemoncello. Lemon Heads? Kidzapalooza All-Stars? Beware! I'm back in it to win it!"

"Wonderful," said Mr. Lemoncello from the broadcast booth. "And you won't be penalized for your, uh, amusing antics with the lightning-bolt blasters."

"Promise?"

"Pinky swear. All is forgiven. Enjoy the rest of the game!"

Charles let go of the lightning-bolt blaster.

He had work to do.

The other players were stranded in the hallways of the Fictionasium or off searching for food.

Maybe they couldn't solve a puzzle in one of their rooms.

Maybe there was no way for them to unlock all five of their locks.

Maybe there was no chance for them to win.

But for Team Charles, the path to victory was clear.

Thanks to his time in the control room, he already knew the answer that would earn him the combination for the Mythology Room's marbled lock.

The final one on his codex!

Charles charged down from Mount Olympus and rushed to the rear of the room, looking for a hologram of the sorceress Circe. She was supposed to be the one to give him his final riddle. (The answer would be "Troy.")

But he couldn't find her.

"Circe? Where are you? Circe?"

The sorceress didn't appear.

Instead, a hologram of a tall and lanky man in wire-rimmed glasses who looked like a jollier version of Charles's father strolled into the room.

"Hello there, Miles."

"What? Who are you?"

"Why, I'm Mr. Millerson."

"You look like my father except you're smiling."

"Heh, heh, heh," laughed the happy man in khakis and a blazer. "I'm smiling, son, because I'm so proud of you."

"What? Why? I haven't won the game yet."

"You know, son, sometimes you learn more from losing than you do from winning. When you lose, you learn how to keep going."

"I don't want to lose! So hurry up and give me a puzzle

or a riddle or a game—something to help me unlock the final lock on my codex!"

"Well, Miles . . ."

"My name isn't Miles! It's Charles! Charles Chiltington! And Chiltingtons never lose!"

Suddenly, the holographic man vanished.

Three deep and throaty growls grumbled out of the darkness.

Five seconds later, Charles was face to face with another monster from Greek mythology.

Cerberus.

The three-headed dog.

51

"That wasn't supposed to happen!" shouted Kyle. "We didn't program a three-headed dog into the scene! Just a dad who sounds more like my dad than Charles's."

"There's a glitch in the computer system!" said Andrew. "Maybe even a virus. I wouldn't be surprised if it started sneezing!"

Kyle and Akimi both rolled their eyes. Andrew hadn't been quite the same since their journey through the Humor Room.

They were all still standing in the hallway, watching the scene inside the Mythology Room play out on the wall-mounted video monitor.

Mr. Lemoncello appeared on the live-feed screen.

"Right now," said Mr. Lemoncello, "viewers everywhere are wondering, 'Was that supposed to happen?'"

"Uh, yeah," said Akimi. "We totally are."

"Well," Mr. Lemoncello told the TV audience, "it seems that Kidzapalooza All-Star Gabrielle Grande, on her junk food journey, ended up in the Narrative Drive supercomputer control room, where our good friend Clarence is known to keep a two-gallon tub of cheese balls. While snacking, Gabrielle grew bored with the jolly Mr. Millerson. So she clicked the mouse and added a new and, I must say, extremely classical element to the mix: Cerberus, the hound of Hades from Greek mythology."

"Whoa," said Haley.

"Should make for a fantastical finish," said Mr. Lemoncello. "One that I have absolutely no control over because I'm still locked out of my own library—with no way to break in!"

"We have to help Charles," said Kyle.

"Why?"

"Because we can."

"Kyle's right," said Haley.

"Um, you guys?" said Akimi, her eyes riveted to the video screen. "It might be too late to help."

Charles was cornered by the beast with the three Rottweiler heads. That meant it had three massive jaws and three sets of drool-dripping fangs. Even though it was just a three-dimensional projection, it was extremely terrifying.

"For Charles to get out of that room," said Sierra, "he's going to need major help from somebody super heroic. Like Hercules."

"We don't have Hercules!" said Akimi.

"True," said Kyle. "But we have Garbageman!"

"Who?" said Haley, because the Kidzapalooza team hadn't spent time in the Comic Book Room of the Fiction-asium.

"Garbageman," said Sierra. "A superhero from sub-urbia."

Kyle started scrolling through character options on the tablet computer again.

"Got him."

"Mix in Granny, that dog with her walker," said Sierra. "Maybe she can gently discipline Cerberus. Or bake him some cookies. Grandmothers are good at both."

"But Charles has stopped firing lightning bolts," said Andrew. "He's back in the game. He's not blowing junk up anymore. The library is safe. That dog is just a hologram. We don't have to help him."

"Yes," said Kyle and Haley, "we do!"

"Let's take a vote," suggested Miguel.

All six hands went up.

"Well, look at that," said Andrew, with his hand raised. "I'm voting against myself. Now, *that's* comedy!"

"Hey, hey, everybody," said Haley, "maybe if we're kind to Charles, he'll be kind to someone else. 'No act of kindness, no matter how small, is ever wasted.'"

"Aha!" said Miguel. "You're quoting Aesop's fables! The one about the lion and the mouse."

"No. I'm quoting last week's episode of *Hey, Hey, Haley*."

"Oooh," said Kyle, tapping the tablet computer screen on the control panel. "A lion and a mouse. Maybe we should toss those into the myth, too!"

"Why not?" said Akimi. "Charles needs all the help he can get!"

52

"Nooooo!" shouted Charles. "Stay away from me!"

The giant dog didn't obey. It prowled closer. Charles could smell its foul, filthy, and fetid breath. It reeked of rotten eggs. Like a gas station bathroom nobody had cleaned in over a century.

"Where's Circe the sorceress?" he demanded. "She's supposed to be here to give me a puzzle!"

"Stand back, young fellow!" a voice boomed behind him.

Charles sniffed the air. Now the sulfurous scent of the underworld had been overwhelmed by the pungent odor of cafeteria compost.

Charles whirled around and saw a dashingly handsome superhero dressed in a crinkly suit made out of trash can liners. He was holding a garbage can lid as his shield.

"I am Garbageman!" the newcomer announced as he

swatted at the flies circling his head. "The superhero of suburbia. And that three-headed hound seems to be in direct violation of this fair burb's canine sanitation laws." He balled up a fist heroically. "Good thing I brought along my pooper-scooper!"

"Your hand?" cried a cranky old dog in a granny bonnet that hobbled into the scene pushing a walker. "Disgusting."

"It's covered in plastic, ma'am," said Garbageman. "Very sanitary."

The dog shooed Garbageman away with a paw. "I'll take care of this, sonny. I speak Dog."

She turned to the snarling beast.

"Cerberus?" barked Granny. "Bad dog. Bad, bad, bad."

The hound opened its triple set of jaws like a trio of spring-loaded bear traps and roared.

"Oh, my!" gasped Granny.

Garbageman immediately leapt between her and the demon dog.

The hound sprang forward, but its heads hit the superhero's garbage-can-lid shield and bounced off.

"Ha!" Garbageman laughed. "That's why they call it a garbage *can*, not a garbage *can't*!"

Cerberus narrowed its coal-red eyes just as a lion, with a mouse riding on its back, leapt out of the shadows.

Cerberus saw the enormous, roaring cat. It loomed larger than life because it was the stuff of fables. The mythical dog knew it had met its match. It turned tail and scuttled away—disappearing when it reached the darkness in the far corner of the room.

Garbageman laughed again. "Well done, noble beast."

The lion bowed majestically. The mouse on its back did the same. Then they silently disappeared.

"You're safe, Charles!" said Garbageman.

Charles heaved a sad sigh. "I guess."

"Why so down in the dumps? That's my job."

"Because I was supposed to get a clue that would help me open the final lock on my codex."

"Ah, yes," said Garbageman. "I have that for you."

Garbageman snapped his fingers. A floating three-dimensional holographic rebus appeared in front of Charles.

It was a puzzle he'd never seen before, because the end of the mythology story had been completely rewritten. He realized that the answer he'd memorized from his time in the control room wouldn't help him open his final lock.

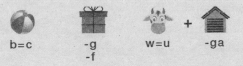

b=c   -g   w=u   +   -ga
           -f

"What the . . . ," mumbled Charles. "It's a rebus. I hate these things."

"Good luck, Charles!" said Garbageman, giving him a

jaunty two-finger salute. "And if you ever wish to join my ranks, remember: There is no official training to become a garbageman. We just pick things up as we go along!"

And with that, Garbageman zoomed toward the ceiling.

"I have to leave, too," said Granny.

"Wait!" cried Charles. "Where's everybody going? I need help. Can't you give me a hint?"

The old dog didn't answer. She just waved and faded away.

"Come back here! Who do you think I am? Some kind of gamer like Kyle Keeley?"

"Don't worry," said a familiar voice.

"The gamers are here to help," said another.

It was Haley Daley and Kyle Keeley.

53

The tips of Charles's ears were turning pink with rage.

"How did you two gain entry to *my* room?" he demanded angrily.

Kyle shrugged. "We came in through the exit."

"We were watching you on the monitor," said Haley.

"Good job defeating the demon dog," said Kyle.

"I didn't do anything!" said Charles. "It was that lion. And the garbageman. And the old dog lady . . ."

"Guess you have more friends than you realize," said Haley.

"Ha! Friends. Do you know what my father says about friends?" Charles glared at Haley. He remembered how she'd double-crossed him during the escape game. "He says, 'Beware of the friend who was once your foe.' "

"Oh-kay," said Haley.

"So, there's, like, fourteen minutes left in the game,"

said Kyle, eyeballing the clock. "Do you need a hand with that rebus, or what?"

Charles gave him a quizzical look. "Why on earth would you ever endeavor to assist, aid, or abet me, Keeley?"

"Come on, Charles," said Haley. "The game's over in fourteen minutes. Let's work the puzzle."

"Yeah," said Kyle. "It's what we gamers do best."

He and Haley focused on the floating images and letters.

" 'Ball,' but 'b' equals 'c,' " said Haley.

" 'Call,' " said Kyle. " 'Gift' minus the 'g' and the 'f.' "

" 'It,' " said Haley.

" 'Courage'!" shouted Charles. "The last word is 'cow,' but the 'w' becomes a 'u,' plus 'garage' without the first 'g' and 'a.' 'Courage'!"

" 'Call it courage'!" said Kyle.

"Okay," said Charles. "It's courage! I called it what you told me to. Now where's my lock combination?"

"Um, you guys?" said Sierra, wandering into the room.

"What's *she* doing here?" demanded Charles.

"Trying to help you," said Akimi, coming into the room behind Sierra. She was followed by Miguel and Andrew.

"Is this some kind of trick?" asked Charles. "I just need to open up one more lock and I win."

"And there's your clue," said Kyle, pointing at the rebus.

"Ha! What kind of clue is that?"

"*Call It Courage* is a novel by Armstrong Sperry," explained Sierra.

"So?" said Charles.

"I believe it won the John Newbery Medal in 1941," said Miguel.

"Big whoop," said Charles.

"How many numbers are on your marble-colored lock?" asked Kyle.

"Four."

"Any four-digit numbers leap to mind?" said Akimi.

"No."

"How about, oh, I don't know, the year?"

Charles reluctantly rotated the lock dial's numbers to the current year.

The lock stayed locked.

"Dumb idea, Akimi."

"Hey, Charles," said Haley. "Try one, nine, four, one."

"Why?"

"Because that's the year *Call It Courage* won the Newbery," said Sierra.

"Another dumb idea," muttered Charles as he nevertheless rotated the dials to 1-9-4-1.

The marble lock flashed a swirl of colors and immediately sprang open.

"Oh, yeah!" thundered the voice in the ceiling. "Final lock? Open! It's breakout time!"

Charles practically ripped the cover off his codex. "Yes! There's an L-shaped key hidden inside!"

The phone in his pocket started vibrating again.

He turned around and snuck a quick peek at the screen to read the message from his father:

FINISH THE JOB!

Charles slipped the phone back into his pocket and spun around.

"So long, losers! I'm breaking out of this loony library!"

"Not so fast, Charles," boomed Mr. Lemoncello's voice from the ceiling speakers.

"Now what?" Kyle wondered aloud.

"Probably another plot twist!" said Miguel.

54

"Goodness gracious gollywhoppers!" Mr. Lemoncello exclaimed. "We now have a three-way tie, much like the one my aunt Rose gave me for Christmas one year!"

"That's right," said Dr. Zinchenko, picking up the color commentary in the broadcast booth. "All three teams, or what remains of them, have opened their codexes. All three have a shiny L-shaped key. All three are still in the game!"

"That means we need to do a Triple-Dripple Super-Duper Tie-Breaker!" cried Mr. Lemoncello.

Bells rang, sirens WHOOPed, and the audience in the town square went wild. The walls of the Fictionasium slid away to reveal the gurgling statue of Mr. Lemoncello and the back of the library's bank vault front door.

"This tie-breaker round has automatically reconfigured the lock on the front door. Two keys will no longer open it. Only one. The one belonging to whichever team cracks the final, tie-breaking puzzle, which, much like my steam-powered mustache curler, we never thought we'd need. Jimmy? Bring in our missing contestant."

"Right you are, Mr. Lemoncello!" thundered the jolly off-camera announcer. "Gabrielle Grande? Please join us in the lobby!"

A rush of prerecorded applause rustled out of the speakers.

"Mr. Lemoncello?" Haley called out.

"Yes, Haley?"

"Can I join the Lemon Heads team?"

"Your wish, as always, is my command. Haley Daley, you are now a Lemon Head."

"Six against one?" moaned Charles. "That's not fair!"

"Maybe you'd like to join the Lemon Heads, too, Charles?"

"No way. I want to defeat them. I want to destroy and demolish and annihilate them, too!" He turned to face his foes. "You fools never should've helped me! You're nothing but a bunch of losers."

"Especially Haley!" snarked Gabrielle as she marched into the lobby, licking orange cheese gunk off her fingertips. "She doesn't have what it takes to be a star."

"She switched sides," said Charles. "She's on Keeley's team now."

"Fine. Then I'll be on yours."

"Really?"

"Yep. I want to beat these chumps even worse than you do. Especially Haley Daley."

"Deal!"

Sirens WHOOPed. "Oh, yeah," said the video game voice. "New teams. Final round. Time for a breakout tie-breaker."

"And now," said Mr. Lemoncello from the broadcast booth, "here's your quizmaster, straight from the Bronze Age, the heavy metal me!"

The Mr. Lemoncello statue in the fountain stopped spewing water, shook its head, and dried off its waistcoat. "I'm such a dribbler," it said.

"Whoa," said Miguel. "The statue is an audio-animatronic dummy, too."

"Oh, really?" said the robotic Mr. Lemoncello, wiggling its bronze eyebrows. "We'll soon see who the real dummies are! I will give you one last puzzle. Solve it, and you're breaking out of the library. Jimmy? Tell them about their prizes!"

"You bet I will, Mr. Metallic Lemoncello!" crooned the game show announcer. "One of our lucky winners is on his or her way to hosting their own Lemoncello game show, right here on the Kidzapalooza Network—where kids rule!"

"It'll probably be me," said Gabrielle, waving at the cameras. "Haley's not ready for another gig. She can barely handle the show she has now."

"Gabby's just jealous," Sierra whispered to Haley. "You're a much better singer than she is."

"What are you people whispering about over there?" demanded Gabrielle.

"Nothing," said Kyle.

"The winner's teammates," the announcer continued, "will become the very first contestants on this all-new, all-exciting game show—eligible for prizes of up to one million dollars!"

"Chuck?" Gabrielle said under her breath. "When we win, I'm hosting the show. You can be my first contestant."

"Do you promise I'll win that game, too? On TV?"

"Absolutely."

Charles turned to the statue. "Bring it, Tin Man!"

55

"Here we go," said the real Mr. Lemoncello, speaking through the statue. "It all comes down to this. The final puzzle!"

Drums rolled.

Lights blinked and strobed.

The crowd in the town square grew hushed.

Kyle's competitive juices were flowing like crazy.

"Our final puzzle comes straight out of my new What Else Do You See? online puzzle game, filled with fast-flipping, high-flying animated optical illusions."

"Available only from Mr. Lemoncello's Imagination Factory," crooned Jimmy the announcer.

Kyle and his friends exchanged excited glances. They'd played this game before. On the computers in the middle school library.

The Mr. Lemoncello statue popped open its pocket

watch. A projector beam streamed out of the round case, creating a floating holographic image of a beautiful woman wearing a crown.

"Behold this fair princess," Mr. Lemoncello said through his statue. "I believe she was crowned at the county fair. Be that as it may, how can you turn this young woman into an old lady in an instant?"

Gabrielle answered fast:

"Make her watch *Hey, Hey, Haley*! That'll age anybody!"

Charles turned to his teammate. "Seriously? That's your answer?"

Gabrielle shrugged. "Whatevs."

"I'm sorry, Ms. Grande," said Mr. Lemoncello. "That answer is extremely incorrect. It is also extremely rude. Lemon Heads? Your answer?"

Kyle and his teammates huddled together to brainstorm.

"What do you guys think?" whispered Kyle.

"That Gabrielle isn't very nice," said Akimi.

"I mean about the puzzle."

"I've seen this one before," said Haley. "Just flip it over."

"Huh?" said Kyle.

"Flip it!"

Kyle turned his head as upside down as he could and tried to see the puzzle the way Haley had already seen it.

"Wow," he said. "You're super smart. I used to think you were just, you know, a cheerleader."

"Kyle?"

"Yeah?"

"Nobody is just one thing."

"Flip?" Kyle said to his other teammates. "Team answer?"

Sierra, Haley, Miguel, Andrew, and Akimi nodded.

"Go for it, bro," said Miguel. "There's only three minutes left on the clock!"

Kyle faced the Mr. Lemoncello statue. "To turn the young girl into an old lady," he said, "you just have to flip the image."

"Final answer?"

"Final answer!"

The Mr. Lemoncello statue waited.

Then it twirled a mustache tip.

And waited some more.

Finally, the statue and the sound effects exploded.

"Correctomundo!"

Bells *DING-DING-DING*ed. Whistles *WHOOP*ed.

The holographic image flipped itself upside down, turning the young girl into an old crone.

Balloons fell from the ceiling—a blizzard of confetti, too.

"Oh, yeah!" boomed the video game voice. "Winner, winner. Chicken dinner."

"We have a winner, ladies and gentlemen!" said the real Mr. Lemoncello, breaking out of the metal statue as if it were a hollow chocolate bunny. "The Lemon Heads, with special guest star Haley Daley!"

"How'd you . . . ," marveled Miguel.

"Easy!" said Mr. Lemoncello, winking at the camera. "All my secret tunnels have secret tunnels! And Mr. Raymo finally figured out how to override that lockdown. Stay tuned, folks. We'll be right back after one last commercial!"

56

"Everybody?" said Kyle, calling his team together for a quick postgame conference. "I think Haley should be the star of the game show. The rest of us can be her first contestants."

"Definitely," said Akimi.

Miguel, Andrew, and Sierra agreed.

"Are you guys sure?" said Haley, wiping confetti flecks off her shoulder.

"Yeah," said Kyle. "We're more into playing games than hosting them."

Suddenly, the audience applauded. Music swelled. The game show was back on the air.

"Lemon Heads?" said Mr. Lemoncello as a camera pushed in for a close-up. "We only have one minute left before Kai Kumar slips and slimes his way through an all-new episode of *Sludge Dodgers*. So let's make like an

Accelerated Reader and be quick: Who from your team will break out of the library first and go on to host their own Lemoncello game show on Kidzapalooza?"

Kyle looked to his friends.

"Haley Daley!" they all shouted.

"Thanks, you guys," said Haley, showing off her trademark sparkle.

Gabrielle Grande shook her head and stormed off the set.

"How do I get out of here?" she demanded, nearly tripping on the curb of the fountain's reflecting pool.

Charles stomped after her.

Suddenly, there was a buzzing sound.

Charles reached into the pocket of his MoCap suit and pulled out his phone.

He glanced at the screen.

"Ah, go win your own games, Father!"

He tossed the phone into the fountain.

The security guards, Clarence and Clement, emerged from the shadows and, each one gently taking an elbow, guided the two angry losers to an alternate exit.

All the cameras were focused on Haley.

She pulled out the L-shaped key and marched to the bank vault door.

The key easily slid into one of the slots. Haley turned it sharply to the right. A resounding thud echoed inside the heavy metal casing.

The massive door swung open.

Strobing lights chased each other around its circular edge.

Haley stepped out onto the porch.

The crowd roared. Balloons fell. Doves were released. A squadron of jets streaked across the sky.

"Haley Daley?" said Mr. Lemoncello as he joined her for the game show's closing two-shot. "You were the first to break out of Mr. Lemoncello's library! You're on your way to hosting a new breakout hit, right here on Kidza-palooza!"

"Where kids rule!" shouted Haley.

Then she ducked.

Because she figured someone was going to heave a pie at her.

They did.

It hit Mr. Lemoncello instead.

"Mmm," he said, wiping his face and licking his fingers. "Lemon meringue. My favorite."

Kyle and his teammates stepped through the door to join Haley and Mr. Lemoncello.

The crowd in the town square roared even louder.

"Way to go, baby bro!" hollered Mike.

"That's my Kyle!" shouted his father. "Way to play, kiddo!"

"Where's Charles?" screamed Mrs. Chiltington. "Charles, dear? Don't worry! Mummy's here!"

"Right this way, Mrs. Chiltington," said a production assistant. "Charles is in his dressing room."

"Did you people lower his self-esteem again?"

When she was gone, Haley led the procession down the steps and into the adoring crowd. Kyle, Akimi, Sierra, Miguel, and Andrew followed her.

Hugs and high fives were exchanged all around. Haley signed autographs and posed for selfies. Mr. Lemoncello licked pie filling off his face.

End credits and titles scrolled over the happy scene.

The TV show was over, but the victory celebration had just begun.

There was food in the town square. Lots of it. Hot dogs, hamburgers, veggie burgers, and barbecue. Potato salad, egg salad, and salad salad. There was cake, as well as more pie and even festive glazed doughnuts.

As the TV crews broke down the broadcast booth and started packing up their equipment, Kyle found Mr. Lemoncello, Dr. Zinchenko, and Mr. Raymo clustered near the doughnuts. He wanted to ask them about the lightning-bolt blasters in the Mythology Room.

"Charles could've destroyed the library," said Kyle.

"Indubitably," said Mr. Lemoncello. "But thanks to you and your friends, he did not. What some might see as a near disaster, I prefer to call marvelous good fortune. This is why the thesaurus has always been my favorite book. So many different ways of looking at the same thing!"

BONG! BONG!

Mr. Lemoncello's top hat started chiming like a church steeple.

"Oh, d-d-dear," he said, his cheeks wiggling in time to the tintinnabulation of the bells inside his hat. "It's m-m-my head phone."

The hat's lid popped open. A yellow telephone attached to a springy cord shot up into the air as far as the coiled wire could stretch, then rubber-banded itself back down into Mr. Lemoncello's hand.

"Nyello?" he said into the phone. "This is Mr. Lemoncello. How may I be of assistance? . . . What? . . . Is that next weekend? . . . Huzzah!"

He covered the phone's mouthpiece with one hand and turned to Kyle. "I must depart Ohio immediately!"

"Why?" asked Kyle.

"I need to be in upstate New York. Next weekend is my annual company picnic at the factory where we manufacture all my amazing games. Oh, those good people are in for a truly spectacularific surprise this year!"

"All is in readiness, sir," said Dr. Zinchenko.

"We've been working on it for months," added Mr. Raymo.

"What is it?" Kyle asked eagerly.

"Ah, if we told you, it wouldn't be a surprise. But, Kyle?"

"Yes?"

"I'll give you a hint: There will be balloons!"

Is the Game Really Over?

Over?

Hello? It's a Lemoncello!

There has to be one more puzzle. It's in the book but not in the story, although the story holds a very big clue about how to solve it. If you crack the code, send your answer to author@ChrisGrabenstein.com to find out if you're correct!

Congratulations to:

Joshua Bernheisel

Ryan Capruso

Hannah Chung

Mirabai Keshap

Kai Kumar

They all solved the hidden puzzle in *Mr. Lemoncello's Great Library Race.* That's how they ended up as characters in this book!

And Alexandra Paisley is on WAMS-TV because she was the winner of the first Welcome to Wonderland trivia contest.

Author's Note

Just this week, I have been a fallen Greek god, a president of the United States, a boy wizard ("the one who lived"), and a young sprinter who nicknamed himself "Ghost."

Because just this week, I've been reading and experiencing fiction: Rick Riordan's *The Hidden Oracle* (The Trials of Apollo series), Bill Clinton and James Patterson's *The President Is Missing,* Broadway's *Harry Potter and the Cursed Child,* and Jason Reynolds's *Ghost.*

For me, that is the true power of fiction: the chance to become someone else for a few hundred pages—or in the case of the Broadway show, five hours.

Fiction, I think, is the world's greatest tool for teaching empathy—the ability to understand and share the feelings of another. It's why I had Sierra Russell quote Atticus Finch from *To Kill a Mockingbird:* "You never really understand a person until you consider things from his point of view . . . until you climb into his skin and walk around in it."

For three books in the Lemoncello series, Charles Chiltington has been protagonist Kyle Keeley's number one nemesis. I thought it was time, in this book, for Kyle to reach a better understanding of what makes Charles act the way he does. I created Mr. Lemoncello's Fictionasium to give Kyle a chance to "consider things" from Charles's point of view. To "climb into his skin and walk around in it."

Some writing instructor (or book on "How to Write a Book") once taught me that villains are the heroes of their own stories. Nobody wakes up every morning, curls the tips of their waxed mustache, and cackles, "Mwah-ha-ha, I am going to be *evil* today!" There is a reason bad guys in stories act badly.

After Kyle walks a mile in Charles's shoes (probably penny loafers), he understands why Charles acts the way he does. Kyle empathizes with Charles. They may never become best friends, but Kyle has a better grasp of what makes his longtime foe such a Chiltington.

I also wanted the other members of Kyle's team, our friends from the previous books, to read outside their comfort zones. For Sierra, it's comic books. For Miguel (and probably me), it's books about sports. For Akimi, it's fairy tales. For Andrew, it's humor—the kind filled with fart jokes. After forcing themselves to enter a genre they might not ordinarily have chosen, they find that their worlds expand in small ways—another great power of fiction.

People much smarter than I have used the metaphor of "mirrors, windows, and sliding glass doors" when discussing fiction—which is, of course, why those are the architectural entry points to Mr. Lemoncello's Fiction-asium. Children's literature scholar Dr. Rudine Sims Bishop, winner of the 2017 Coretta Scott King–Virginia Hamilton Award for Lifetime Achievement for her work related to African American children's literature, created this succinct "mirror, window, door" metaphor in a 1990 essay:

> *Books are sometimes windows, offering views of worlds that may be real or imagined, familiar or strange. These windows are also sliding glass doors, and readers have only to walk through in imagination to become part of whatever world has been created or re-created by the author. . . . A window can also be a mirror. Literature transforms human experience and reflects it back to us, and in that reflection, we can see our own lives and experiences as part of the larger human experience.*[1]

And, of course, one reader's mirror might become another reader's window or sliding glass door.

A chance to become someone else for a few hundred pages.

To climb into their skin and walk around in it.

To learn more about what it means to be fully human.

---

1. Rudine Sims Bishop, "Mirrors, Windows, and Sliding Glass Doors," *Perspectives: Choosing and Using Books for the Classroom,* vol. 6, no. 3 (Summer 1990).

Mr. Lemoncello's All-Star Breakout Game Reading List

Here's a complete list of the works mentioned or alluded to in *Mr. Lemoncello's All-Star Breakout Game*. How many have *you* read?

- ❏ *The Adventures of Sherlock Holmes* by Sir Arthur Conan Doyle
- ❏ *Aesop's Fables*
- ❏ *Alexander and the Terrible, Horrible, No Good, Very Bad Day* by Judith Viorst
- ❏ *Alice's Adventures in Wonderland* by Lewis Carroll
- ❏ *Artemis Fowl* by Eoin Colfer
- ❏ *The Art of War* by Sun Tzu
- ❏ *Bad Magic* by Pseudonymous Bosch
- ❏ "The Bells" by Edgar Allan Poe
- ❏ *Bud, Not Buddy* by Christopher Paul Curtis
- ❏ *Call It Courage* by Armstrong Sperry
- ❏ *Captains Courageous* by Rudyard Kipling
- ❏ Captain Underpants series by Dav Pilkey
- ❏ *Charlotte's Web* by E. B. White
- ❏ *Counting by 7s* by Holly Goldberg Sloan
- ❏ *Creepy Carrots!* by Aaron Reynolds
- ❏ *The Crossover* by Kwame Alexander
- ❏ *The Day the Crayons Quit* by Drew Daywalt and Oliver Jeffers

- *Dead End in Norvelt* by Jack Gantos
- Diary of a Wimpy Kid series by Jeff Kinney
- Eloise series by Kay Thompson
- Encyclopedia Brown series by Donald J. Sobol
- *The Epic Fail of Arturo Zamora* by Pablo Cartaya
- *Frankenstein* by Mary Shelley
- *From the Mixed-Up Files of Mrs. Basil E. Frankweiler* by E. L. Konigsburg
- *Ghost* by Jason Reynolds
- *The Girl Who Drank the Moon* by Kelly Barnhill
- *The Gollywhopper Games* by Jody Feldman
- Goosebumps series by R. L. Stine
- Hardy Boys series by Franklin W. Dixon
- Harry Potter series by J. K. Rowling
- *Hello, Universe* by Erin Entrada Kelly
- *If You Give a Mouse a Cookie* by Laura Numeroff and Felicia Bond
- *Inside Out and Back Again* by Thanhha Lai
- *The Island of Dr. Libris* by Chris Grabenstein
- *Julius Caesar* by William Shakespeare
- *The Jumbies* by Tracey Baptiste
- Junie B. Jones series by Barbara Park
- *Laugh Out Loud* by James Patterson and Chris Grabenstein
- *The Little Engine That Could* by Watty Piper
- *Long Way Down* by Jason Reynolds
- *The Lord of the Rings* by J. R. R. Tolkien
- *Make Way for Ducklings* by Robert McCloskey

- ❑ Mary Poppins series by P. L. Travers
- ❑ Maximum Ride series by James Patterson
- ❑ *The Miraculous Journey of Edward Tulane* by Kate DiCamillo
- ❑ The Mysterious Benedict Society series by Trenton Lee Stewart
- ❑ Nancy Drew series by Carolyn Keene
- ❑ *Oh, the Places You'll Go!* by Dr. Seuss
- ❑ Percy Jackson and the Olympians series by Rick Riordan
- ❑ *Percy Jackson's Greek Gods* by Rick Riordan
- ❑ *Peter Nimble and His Fantastic Eyes* by Jonathan Auxier
- ❑ *Peter Pan* by J. M. Barrie
- ❑ "The Pit and the Pendulum" by Edgar Allan Poe
- ❑ "The Purloined Letter" by Edgar Allan Poe
- ❑ *The Red Badge of Courage* by Stephen Crane
- ❑ *Roller Girl* by Victoria Jamieson
- ❑ *Sammy Keyes and the Hotel Thief* by Wendelin Van Draanen
- ❑ *A Snicker of Magic* by Natalie Lloyd
- ❑ *The Snowy Day* by Ezra Jack Keats
- ❑ *The Stars Beneath Our Feet* by David Barclay Moore
- ❑ *The Stinky Cheese Man and Other Fairly Stupid Tales* by Jon Scieszka and Lane Smith
- ❑ Tales of Magic series by Edward Eager
- ❑ *Three Times Lucky* by Sheila Turnage
- ❑ *To Kill a Mockingbird* by Harper Lee

- *Turtle in Paradise* by Jennifer L. Holm
- *The Watsons Go to Birmingham—1963* by Christopher Paul Curtis
- *Where the Mountain Meets the Moon* by Grace Lin
- *Where the Sidewalk Ends* by Shel Silverstein
- *Wonder* by R. J. Palacio
- *The Wonderful Wizard of Oz* by L. Frank Baum
- *A Year Down Yonder* by Richard Peck

Hearty and Splendiferous Thank-Yous!

Mr. Lemoncello has Dr. Zinchenko, Mr. Raymo, Clarence, Clement, and the entire staff of his Imagination Factory. I am lucky to have my own incredible crew. None of these Lemoncello books would have been possible without the extraordinarily fantabulous help of so many dedicated people. (So. Many. People.)

Thank you to . . .

My extremely talented wife, J.J. She reads everything first and is absolutely amazing in her critiques. (We should write a book together someday!)

My longtime literary agent and a dapper man-about-town, Eric Myers.

My fantastic editor at Random House, Shana Corey. There is no one I'd rather tell a story with. She is more than ably assisted by the wonderful Polo Orozco, who helps in so many ways (like figuring out all the books mentioned in this book).

The awesometastic art department folks who make these books look so good, inside and out: Michelle Cunningham, Katrina Damkoehler, Nicole de las Heras, Maria

Middleton, Stephanie Moss, Trish Parcell, Larsson McSwain and Martha Rago.

James Lancett, who has created all four amazing and iconic covers in the series.

The keen-eyed copyeditors who make sure my punctuation and grammar are much better than they were on my SATs: Barbara Bakowski and Alison Kolani.

The wondermous production team, headed up by Tim Terhune.

Mr. Lemoncello's many, many friends at Random House Children's Books: John Adamo, Kerri Benvenuto, Julianne Conlon, Janet Foley, Judith Haut, Kate Keating, Jules Kelly, Kim Lauber, Gillian Levinson, Mallory Loehr, Barbara Marcus, Kelly McGauley, Michelle Nagler, and Janine Perez.

The marvelous and matchless school and library team at RHCB: Stevie Durocher, Lisa Nadel, Kristin Schulz, and Adrienne Waintraub.

My pals in publicity: Dominique Cimina, Aisha Cloud, and Noreen Herits.

The sensational sales force, who do such a great job getting the right books into the right kids' hands: Joe English, Bobbie Ford, Felicia Frazier, Becky Green, Kimberly Langus, Deanna Meyeroff, Sarah Nasif, Mark Santella, and Richard Vallejo.

The teachers and librarians all over the country who constantly amaze me with their creativity as they make books come to life for even their most reluctant readers.

And a tip of the hat to Tom Carrozza and all my friends from the First Amendment, a comedy and improv troupe that once upon a time, way back in the early 1980s, saw Garbageman (me), the superhero of suburbia, first take flight with his comrade-in-arms Fireman (Tom).

Welcome!
For the first time, you are invited INSIDE Mr. Lemoncello's one-of-a-kind Gameworks Factory!

Far away from Mr. Lemoncello's magical library, everyone's favorite game maker is building something new. Something SECRET. And he's about to let the world see.

With the help of Kyle and the Lemoncello All-Stars, four lucky boys and girls will win the chance to be among the very first inside. There, the winning kids will go on a Lemoncello-tastic scavenger hunt adventure that will test their skills and their wits, taking them through larger-than-life live-action games—dizzying Chutes and Ladders, death-defying games of Rush Hour, and much, much more!

But the real secret? Deep inside the new building, Mr. Lemoncello has hidden a single ticket. A titanium ticket. Each game will get the players closer to the ticket. And whoever finds the ticket will be eligible to compete for a prize beyond their wildest dreams!

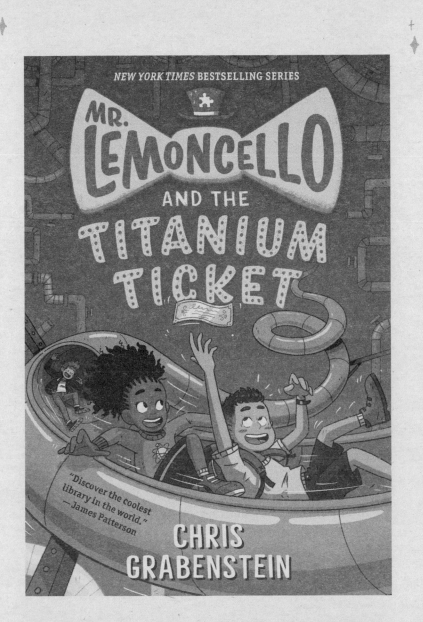

NEW YORK TIMES BESTSELLING SERIES

MR. LEMONCELLO
AND THE
TITANIUM TICKET

"Discover the coolest library in the world."
—James Patterson

CHRIS GRABENSTEIN

TURN THE PAGE TO START READING!

PROLOGUE

"There goes that clock again!" said Akimi Hughes as, off in the distance, four musical notes chimed three separate times. "We only have fifteen minutes left. Hurry!"

"I'm hurrying!" said Kyle Keeley.

"Hurry faster."

Kyle and Akimi had traveled from their homes in Ohio to help the world-famous game maker Mr. Luigi L. Lemoncello, test out a brand-new, supersecret interactive gaming experience that would soon have its gala grand opening in Hudson Hills, New York—a town Kyle and Akimi had always dreamed of visiting.

Because Hudson Hills was where Mr. Lemoncello made all his games!

During the day, they'd toured the unbelievably amazing factory and eaten peanut butter pie with marshmallow and chocolate sauce in the company cafeteria. Tonight, they'd spent two hours running around inside a mysterious world of puzzles, games, and holographic surprises—piecing together a cryptic message on a tablet computer.

"Here comes our final riddle," said Kyle.

A string of letters scrolled across the video screen in the dashboard of the miniature amusement-park car they were sitting in.

"Oh, joy," said Akimi. "This only makes, what? Eight of 'em?"

Kyle glanced down at the tablet's screen. He and Akimi needed to enter their response to the riddle in a series of letter bubbles, spaced to represent words, just like in the game hangman. Some of the bubbles had numbers underneath them.

OO O OOOOOOOO OOOO
25 13   50   16   70

"Okay," said Kyle, "this is going to be a four-word answer. Two letters, one letter, eight letters, four letters."

"This is also the most complicated game Mr. Lemoncello ever created!" said Akimi.

"Because the prize is huge," said Kyle. "A titanium ticket! Titanium's better than gold, right?"

"Totally," said Akimi.

"But what's it a ticket *for*?" wondered Kyle.

"Something bigger than big, or Mr. Lemoncello wouldn't've flown us here on his private jet to test it!"

"You're right! Okay. Here's our riddle: 'When can you jump over three men without getting up?'"

"Duh. Easy," said Akimi. "'In a checkers game.' Two letters, one letter, eight letters, four letters. Ka-boom!"

Kyle tapped in Akimi's answer. The letters in the numbered bubbles automatically appeared in the corresponding numbered spaces in the phrase that Kyle and Akimi had been slowly piecing together as they worked their way through eight different game stations.

"Excellent," said Kyle, watching the computer do its thing and slide the numbered letters into the appropriate positions. "'I' is going to twenty-five, 'N' to thirteen, 'C' to fifty . . ."

"Um, Kyle? I can see the screen. I don't need a play-by-play."

Kyle and Akimi had been best friends forever—even before they started winning all sorts of games together inside Mr. Lemoncello's library, back home in Ohio. But a ticking time clock could strain even the tightest of friendships. Right now, they were a guitar string—one tuning-peg twist away from snapping.

The tablet computer blared a triumphant, if tinny, trumpet fanfare.

"Yes!" said Kyle. "With that answer, we have officially filled in the whole phrase."

Kyle and Akimi climbed out of the cramped little red car they had successfully maneuvered through a massive traffic jam of brightly colored vehicles that had blocked them in. A soothing female voice purred from hidden ceiling speakers: "Congratulations, KYLE and AKIMI. You have successfully completed all eight games."

"Yes!" said Kyle, with an arm pump.

"Booyah!" added Akimi, slapping him a high five.

"Good luck with the rest of your quest," said the recorded voice. "We hope you make it to the finals."

Kyle and Akimi stared at each other.

Finally, Akimi exploded. "The rest of our quest? We're not done? We filled in the whole phrase!"

"What 'finals' is she talking about?" added Kyle.

"You have seven minutes remaining," cooed the calm voice.

"To do what?" Akimi shouted at the ceiling.

Kyle's mind was spinning. Racing. "Maybe there's a hidden code in the phrase." He looked back at the game screen. "Hang on." Sixteen letters in the final phrase started glowing, the circles behind them turning into fluorescent-yellow lemons.

"We've got glowing letters," he reported. "G-E-C-E-C-D-E-D-C-D-G-D-C-E-G. And another 'G.'"

"You think it's some kind of anagram?" asked Akimi.

"Maybe," said Kyle. "We should figure out all the words we can make with those sixteen letters."

"Good idea! Um, 'deeded,'" said Akimi. "'Ceded,' 'edged,' 'egg' . . ."

"Egg!" said Kyle. "Mr. Lemoncello probably hid an Easter egg somewhere in one of these rooms."

"Easter was a while ago, Kyle. The egg would be rotten by now. We would've smelled it."

"In video games, an Easter egg isn't a real egg; it's an inside joke," he explained. "A hidden message . . ."

Akimi looked around. "Oh. So how do we find it?"

"I have no idea."

"Wait!" said Akimi. "Maybe it's a substitution code, where every letter stands for a different letter! Mr. Lemoncello has done that before."

"You're right! But we need some sort of clue to know how many letters to skip ahead in the alphabet."

Akimi snapped her fingers. "There's a license plate on the back of this car!"

She scurried around to the rear bumper.

"What's the number?" asked Kyle.

"Three!"

Kyle tried to think faster than fast. "Okay, we jump ahead three letters in the alphabet."

"Or we could count three backward," said Akimi. "After all, this is the *rear* bumper!"

"Let's do forward first."

"Fine."

Kyle started at the beginning of the string of glowing letters.

" 'J' is three letters past 'G' . . ."

" 'E' becomes 'H,' " said Akimi. " 'C' becomes 'F' . . ."

"And 'D' becomes 'G'!" added Kyle.

"So," wondered Akimi, "does that mean 'D' becomes 'J,' too? Because if 'D' is 'G' and 'G' is 'J' . . ."

"Why are there only four different letters?" shouted Kyle. "Why aren't any of them vowels?"

" 'E' used to be a vowel!" Akimi shouted back. "Until you made me turn it into an 'H'!"

"You're the one who did that!" countered Kyle.

"Because you told me to! I knew we should've gone backward!"

Off in the distance, clock chimes played their hourly melody and started tolling.

It was nine o'clock.

"Sorry," said the voice in the ceiling. "Your quest remains incomplete. You lose."

"We lost?" Kyle groaned.

"Only because *this is impossible!*" screamed Akimi.

Suddenly, she heard a series of familiar, high-pitched burp-squeaks. A hologram of Mr. Lemoncello, dressed all in black except for his bright-yellow banana shoes, stepped out of the shadows.

"Impossible?" he said. "Oh, it's possible. But for a prize this humongous, I'm afraid the final puzzle must be magnifficult: which is to say, magnificently difficult! Because whosoever solves it will automatically win a titanium ticket and move on to the final round!"

"The final round of what, sir?" Kyle asked politely. He'd loved Mr. Lemoncello since forever, but sometimes . . .

"Sorry," the hologram replied with a sly wink. "I can't tell you. Not yet, anyway. For, you see, good friends, the final round will be the most important game ever played in the history of gaming! Because the winner will become an instant bazillionaire!"

It was after nine o'clock on a school night.

Simon Skrindle, a short (and nearly invisible) seventh grader at Hudson Hills Middle School, had just crept out of the dark forest near the Lemoncello Gameworks Factory.

He was a twelve-year-old on a mission.

He was alone. Simon didn't have many friends, especially not the kind who'd go on an adventure with him, sneaking through the woods late at night.

And this was a BIG adventure.

Simon was going to be the first to see what secrets were hidden inside the new building *behind* Mr. Lemoncello's factory!

For twenty-five years, Luigi L. Lemoncello, the world-famous game maker, had manufactured his games inside the fantastical castle fortress of the Lemoncello

Gameworks—a sprawling factory perched high on a hilltop overlooking the Hudson River. Its four corner towers looked like upside-down snow cones made out of lemon-yellow oval bricks. The pinnacles at their pointy tips were topped with cello weather vanes. Sculptures of game pieces served as gargoyles. The factory's water tower was a one-million-gallon lemon on stilts. During the day, enormous smokestacks puffed out billowy clouds of steam in the shapes of animals or famous faces. Simon loved seeing the Abraham Lincoln and George Washington clouds drifting across the sky over the factory every Presidents' Day. And the bunnies at Easter time. People came from all over to take selfies with the cartoon clouds. Another pipe let out enormous rainbow-colored bubbles every weekend.

There was also a giant ball-pit moat surrounding the whole factory and you could only enter when the drawbridge was lowered. Workers had to know the secret password and shout it into an enormous curled horn that looked like something out of a Dr. Seuss book.

And for the past five years, Mr. Lemoncello had spent a ton of money and time constructing a top secret new building close to his factory fortress. All the work had been done behind forty-foot-tall plywood walls (painted yellow, of course). The workers and contractors and architects had been sworn to secrecy about what they were doing on the other side of that wooden barricade.

Rumors buzzed around the town, anyway.

One guy at school, Jack McClintock, whose dad was the head of security at the Gameworks Factory, said the new building was nothing but a fancy warehouse for "storing junk." A girl in Simon's science class, Soraiya Mitchell, whose father was the plant manager, said the new building would be filled with "amazing twenty-second-century game-making technology."

Basically, nobody knew what was inside the new building. But everybody wanted to find out. Kids at school were even daring each other to "bust in."

No one had the nerve to try.

Then, two weeks ago, the yellow plywood walls came down to reveal a modern, three-story silver box with mirrored walls. At night, those walls reflected back the twinkling black sky.

Plywood down, the secret glass building was now surrounded by three rings of chain-link fences, set up in concentric circles. Each fence had a locked gate, which could be reached by following a footpath from the factory parking lot past a bed of yellow and orange flowers spelling out the word "gesundheit," then on through rows of topiary—evergreen shrubs trimmed to resemble Mr. Lemoncello in various poses (juggling, dancing, tipping an egg timer, balancing a pair of giant dice on his nose). Some kids at school said the fences were electrified, too.

Security for the new building was tight. Super tight.

Simon's grandfather, who hated all things Lemoncello, swore that "the batty old bazillionaire is installing an army of robots in that new building so he can fire all the factory workers!"

Simon's grandpa, Sam Skrindle, had no proof for his theory. It was more or less a wild guess.

That's all anybody in Hudson Hills had. Wild guesses and theories based on even wilder rumors.

So Simon decided *he* would be the first one to actually step foot inside Mr. Lemoncello's secret new building. He'd show the kids at school. He'd take their dare. He'd also take a few pictures with his phone to prove that he'd done it.

Besides, Simon had what his grandmother called "an insatiable curiosity." He loved tearing things apart just to see how they worked. And then he loved putting them back together.

Usually, he could.

Except that one time with his grandmother's blow-dryer. When Simon put it back together, the thing sucked air *in* instead of blowing it *out*. It inhaled her hair like a hungry, hungry hippo slurping spaghetti.

It took a week for the bathroom not to smell like a charred wig.

Fortunately, his grandmother wasn't upset. She laughed and said, "Yep, just like your father."

Simon's grandparents were some of the few adults in the whole town who had never, ever worked at the Gameworks Factory. Mr. Lemoncello was the main employer in Hudson Hills. Had been for twenty-five years. Everybody said he paid the best wages in the world and had the best benefits, too—medical, dental, free books, a rock climbing wall, two zero-gravity rooms, plus an indoor archery range *and* a bowling alley.

Everybody in Hudson Hills loved the zany game maker.

Everybody except Simon's grandfather, who said the meanest, nastiest, ugliest things about Mr. Lemoncello—at the grocery store, at the hardware store, at the barbershop, in letters to the local newspaper, even after church on Sundays.

Sam Skrindle was the town kook.

Maybe that's why Simon didn't have very many friends.

And why he had to break into the secret building!

If he did, he'd prove to all the kids at school that not everybody in Hudson Hills named Skrindle was a total joke.

Simon scurried across the moonlit lawn, past a topiary trimmed to look like Mr. Lemoncello floss dancing, and made it to the pathway, which he followed to the first of the three locked gates.

There was a small metal box mounted on it. Inside the box, Simon discovered a thumbprint scanner, a video screen, and a keypad. He figured the scanner was for authorized workers. Everybody else probably needed to tap in some kind of security code to open the lock.

A recorded voice said, "Greetings and salutations!"

It was Mr. Lemoncello himself!

Mr. Lemoncello didn't visit Hudson Hills all that much, but Simon recognized his voice from TV commercials and the *All-Star Breakout Game* on the Kidzapalooza Network.

"To enter this supersecret zone," the recorded voice continued, "puzzletastic skills must be shown!"

A riddle scrolled across the video screen: *There are 100 bricks on a plane. One falls off. How many are left?*

Simon thought about that. He wondered if it was a trick question. *It couldn't be this easy.* Then he shrugged and tapped 99 on the keypad.

A flashing *Correct!* filled the screen and dissolved into animated fireworks. The pixels rearranged themselves to create a new question: *What are the three steps for putting an elephant into a refrigerator?*

What? Simon thought. He knew Mr. Lemoncello was wacky, but this question was just plain weird.

"It'd have to be a jumbo-sized fridge," he mumbled. Then he thought out the logical steps. *One, open the door. Two, put the elephant in. Three, close the door.* It made sense, so he typed those three steps on the keypad.

"Oh, what fun!" boomed Mr. Lemoncello's recorded voice. "You have opened lock number one!"

There was a solid *CLUNK* of a latch springing free. The gate creaked open an inch. Simon pushed it the rest of the way and hurried down the yellow brick walkway to the second gate, where he found a second puzzle box.

Another question glowed on its screen: *What are the four steps for putting a giraffe in a refrigerator?*

Simon started to type in the same answer that he'd just given for the elephant/fridge question.

Then he stopped.

That was three steps. This question asked for four.

He needed an extra step. He rubbed the short, fuzzy

hair on top of his head as if it were a lucky tennis ball. Sometimes head rubbing helped him think. So did humming.

What if it's the same refrigerator? he asked himself. He shrugged again. He took a risk and typed in his answer, even though it felt more like a guess: *One, open the door. Two, take the elephant out. Three, put the giraffe in. Four, close the door.*

The screen remained frozen for a second.

Then it burst into those *Correct!* fireworks again.

The dots pulled themselves together to form another question: *A lion was having a party and he invited the other animals. All of them came except one. Which one was it?*

WHAT WOULD YOU DO IF YOU SUDDENLY BECAME A GENIUS?!

Don't miss Chris Grabenstein's

COMING IN 2020!

"Clever, fast-paced and incredibly funny."
—STUART GIBBS, *New York Times* bestselling author of *Spy School*

Astronauts made it to the moon. Can Piper make it through middle school?

"Who do you want to be?" asks Mr. Van Deusen. "And not when you grow up. Right now."

Shine on! might be the catchphrase of Piper's hero—astronaut, astronomer, and television host Nellie DuMont Frissé—but Piper knows the truth: some people are born to shine, and she's *not* one of them. This fact has never been clearer than now, since her dad's new job has landed them both at Chumley Prep, an exclusive private school where *everyone* seems to be the very best at something . . . and where Piper *definitely* doesn't fit in.

When a mysterious alum launches a new award, the whole school goes into overachieving overdrive to win it. There's no way Piper can compete! Unless . . .

Is Piper finally ready to step out of the shadows? Can she stay true to herself and still find a way to shine?

"*Shine!* more than shines; it GLOWS."

—Wendy Mass, *New York Times* bestselling author of *The Candymakers*

"Inspirational, commonsensical, and a whole lot of fun." —James Patterson

J.J. AND CHRIS GRABENSTEIN

New York Times bestselling author of
Escape from Mr. Lemoncello's Library

SHINE!

In a school
full of stars,
is there room
for one more?

Favorites from Chris Grabenstein

The Island of Dr. Libris
Shine! (coauthored with J.J. Grabenstein)

THE MR. LEMONCELLO'S LIBRARY SERIES
Escape from Mr. Lemoncello's Library
Mr. Lemoncello's Library Olympics
Mr. Lemoncello's Great Library Race
Mr. Lemoncello's All-Star Breakout Game
Mr. Lemoncello and the Titanium Ticket

THE WELCOME TO WONDERLAND SERIES
Home Sweet Motel
Beach Party Surf Monkey
Sandapalooza Shake-Up
Beach Battle Blowout

THE HAUNTED MYSTERY SERIES
The Crossroads
The Demons' Door
The Zombie Awakening
The Black Heart Crypt

COAUTHORED WITH JAMES PATTERSON
The House of Robots series
The I Funny series
The Jacky Ha-Ha series
Katt vs. Dogg
The Max Einstein series
Pottymouth and Stoopid
The Treasure Hunters series
Word of Mouse